Only once have I dreamed of a unicorn. It was a baby, small and plump as a stuffed toy, with a tiny bud of a horn. The little unicorn nestled contentedly in the arms of my younger sister, Lisa. I remember the light that surrounded the unicorn, and how it shone on the little girl's smiling face and blond hair. Lisa held out the unicorn to me, as if to share the magic. And then, the dream was gone.

A lot has changed since that long-ago dream, but even more remains the same. So this book is for you, Lisa. You are more magical than you know.

1

The School of Magic

Korigan stroked the travel-worn map to ease out the wrinkles. With a sigh of longing, he left the classroom behind and daydreamed his way onto the map.

He imagined that the rustling parchment was wind blowing through autumn leaves. Silent as a stag, he stalked through his imaginary forest. Then he ventured out onto the open moor, where the late heather bloomed and his teacher's voice was nothing more than the hum of contented bees. On the far side of the grassy moor loomed the mountains, wild and full of secrets. The Iceflow River wandered through these mountains on its way to distant lands. Korigan traced the thin squiggle of blue ink with a wistful finger and wished with all his heart that he could follow the river.

A sudden jangle of chimes shattered Korigan's dream and thrust him squarely back into the classroom. He glanced out the window toward the noise. In the courtyard stood a large, marble sundial, held aloft by four statues of famous wizards. The brass pipes of a calliope encircled the stone figures like the bars of a cage, and the gaudy musical contraption was wheezing and clanging its way through a silly dance tune.

Like most other things in Sanderstone, the sundial had no business working as well as it did. Proper sundials required sun. Today clouds lay low and thick over the village, and the sky was the pearly gray peculiar to autumn mornings. Korigan hated the unnatural sundial, but his six classmates greeted its chimes with murmurs of relief. With quick, eager fingers they rolled up their maps and prepared to get down to the real business of the school: magic.

"Today's lesson is a spell for throwing fire," announced Rimgor, the lore master. He picked up a small, lumpy sack and a handful of tiny parchment scrolls. Talking all the while, he began passing out the scrolls and the lumps to his students.

Rimgor was a short, potbellied fellow who bore a remarkable resemblance to a set of bagpipes. His coarse brown beard was braided into three plaits that stuck out in odd directions, and a tartan kilt was belted slightly below his armpits and just above the swell of his belly. Although he droned his way through lessons in map lore and history, Rimgor's voice leaped into piercing melody whenever he took interest in his subject. He was fairly singing now as he made the rounds of the classroom.

He stopped by Korigan's desk last, as usual. Since Korigan showed little talent for magic, few of his teachers bothered much with him. Rimgor thrust a scroll at the boy, handed him a stone about the size of a dove's egg, and gave him a few verbal instructions. Korigan tuned out the drone and skirl of the teacher's voice, but he picked up the stone and examined it. It was nothing but common flint.

Korigan sniffed and rolled his eyes skyward.

"What's wrong this time?" inquired a droll whisper on his left.

He turned to face Aileen, his only friend at the wizard school. She was a merry, mischievous girl with sleek brown hair and eyes the color of summer moss.

"Starting a fire with flint!" he muttered scornfully. "For that, you need magic?"

"Not all of us have your skill with forest lore," Aileen pointed out. She reached out to tug at a lock of Korigan's red hair. "Besides, you might be able to *start* fire with flint, but you can't *throw* fire with it!"

She voiced this observation with a gleam in her eye that Korigan knew well and mistrusted completely. Everyone in Sanderstone—everyone but him, that is—seemed to have some sort of special magical talent. Aileen was handy. She built marvelous little devices that ran on the spells she learned in class. More often than not, these magical toys were the centerpiece of some elaborate prank. The very thought of magical fire in her hands made Korigan swallow hard.

He glanced down at the chunk of flint in his hand and was pleased to note that the stone was not completely useless. It was shaped almost like an arrowhead. A little chipping and smoothing would make it just right. Korigan pocketed the stone in the bag that hung from the left side of his belt, where he kept his arrowheads, bits of string, a small knife, feathers for his arrows, and other necessary items. On the right side of his belt hung his spell bag, a small magical sack that sorted and brought to hand whatever object was needed to cast a spell. As Rimgor often said, "When goblins attack, you don't have time to rummage." Korigan had spent almost fifteen years—his entire life—in the village of Sanderstone, and he had never experienced anything like a goblin attack. To his way of thinking, rampaging goblins would be an improvement.

"You may open your scrolls now," announced Rimgor. "On them is written a rune, a word of power that for this spell must be spoken quickly six times. Who can tell me the significance of the number six?"

As another student supplied the answer, Aileen nudged Korigan and leaned in close. "Six. Isn't that the number of toes on a lore master's foot?" she whispered.

Elaine Cunningham

Korigan shot her a quick grin and lifted a finger to his lips in warning.

"Why? We're supposed to practice pronouncing the word of power. As long you *look* studious, you can say whatever you like." Aileen lifted her scroll and furrowed her brow in mock concentration. "Did you know that we're going to get our familiars today?" she murmured from one side of her mouth. "Isn't that good news?"

Good news! Korigan wanted to leap out of his seat and shout for joy. For five years, only the promise of his own familiar—a wizard's animal companion—had sustained him through the absurdity of the School of Magic. Korigan loved animals. He spent many stolen hours in the forest, studying their habits and learning their ways. He'd even raised a falcon hatchling and trained her to hunt. The sleek, fierce Starhawk was his dearest companion, but a *familiar* would be something far more. A wizard and his familiar could speak mind-to-mind, and Korigan would be able to see the world through the eyes of one of the animals he loved.

"What kind of familiar do you suppose I'll get?" Aileen mused. Wizards and familiars were matched in a process that was mysterious to everyone but Spartish, the old man in charge of magical beasts.

"A monkey," Korigan replied without hesitation. "No other animal could match you for mischief!"

The girl pretended to pout, but her eyes danced with anticipation. They had trained for five long years to become apprentice wizards, and they were finally ready to receive their familiars. Next to such a thing, a lesson about throwing fire seemed dull indeed!

At the end of class, Rimgor told the class to report to the Bestiary. His seven students leaped to their feet liked puppets pulled by a single string. Korigan and Aileen, who were always the last to enter the classroom, had the advantage over their more studious classmates. They flew out of the door before the others could even gather up their new spell scrolls.

Side by side the two friends raced down the maze of streets that led to Spartish's domain. They passed the alchemist classroom, a stone building sturdy enough to withstand the many minor explosions that had occurred there over the years. Its tiled roof had been patched so frequently that it looked like a multicolored quilt. Aileen grinned and pointed to a shiny new patch, the latest evidence of her own handiwork. Korigan nodded absently.

"Let's cut through the children's yard!" he suggested. Children who were too young to attend the School of Magic spent their days playing together, so that their parents might tend to magic, the all-important business of Sanderstone. This morning the little ones were clustered around an illusionist, who entertained them with stories of wizards and wondrous beasts. The children were so intent on watching the magical, multicolored shadows act out the story that they hardly noticed Aileen and Korigan dash through their playground.

As the two friends rounded the last corner, the sounds and smells of animals greeted them. Aileen wrinkled her nose, but Korigan was accustomed to the Bestiary. He came here often to watch Spartish at work. As usual, the door was open. Spartish was busy tending a half-grown hound puppy who had just learned that porcupines should be treated with respect and caution.

Korigan looked around the barnlike room with delight. A pair of sleek otters splashed and played in a water trough. A red fox eyed a new family of turkey chicks with professional interest. Ferrets, slim and swift as brown lightning, chased each other up and down the posts and rafters. Two raccoons were busily washing some salted herrings in a pitcher of ale. Korigan grinned. Spartish was so absent-minded that he would probably drink the ale without noticing its new, fishy flavor.

A curious bear waddled over to sniff at the hem of Aileen's gown. The girl froze, and her hand edged toward her spell bag.

"Come in, come in," called Spartish with a touch of impatience. "And you, girl—don't even think about casting a spell in here. Old Barnacle won't bother you unless you get him riled." The old man glanced up, and his scowl became less fierce when he saw Korigan.

"How's the falcon, boy? She got you trained proper yet?"

Spartish always greeted him that way. Korigan doubted that the old man even knew his name. The master of beasts paid closer heed to animals than he did to people, but that was fine with Korigan.

"Starhawk caught two partridges last week," Korigan boasted. "She's fully grown now, and as fast as an arrow!"

"Good, good," Spartish said absently. He turned his attention back to the dog, whose muzzle bristled with quills. Speaking softly all the while, he carefully tugged out the painful barbs. The puppy whimpered a bit as each quill came free, but she held the old man's gaze with eyes full of love and trust. Korigan crouched down to watch, marveling at the bond between man and puppy. Spartish had a way with animals that went far beyond the control spells some of Sanderstone's wizards could cast. Korigan suspected that the old man knew exactly what a squirrel said when it chattered, and that he understood why a hawk loved to fly.

At that moment Korigan's five classmates skidded around the corner. They edged into the Bestiary, their eyes wide with a mixture of fear and excitement as they gazed around the odd room. The bear, who had settled down at Aileen's feet like an overgrown dog, whuffled indignantly and padded off into the far shadows. Aileen heaved a ragged sigh of relief.

"Take a seat on the floor. Make a semicircle. And keep quiet!" Spartish snapped.

At once the students did as they were told. Most people in Sanderstone were a little afraid of Spartish, who made friends with even the oddest and most dangerous animals. As old as he was, he could train the most skittish horse to a saddle, face down a grumpy bear, or talk a skunk out of spraying. Sometimes the students made fun of the strange old man, but they made sure that he never overheard them doing it.

While Korigan waited, he looked around the room and wondered which of the animals might be his familiar. To all appearances, Spartish paid little attention to humans, yet the master usually managed to match each student to the animal best suited to his or her talents. And though Korigan might not be much of a wizard, he loved to hunt, and he was very, very good at it. He wanted a familiar who could roam the forest with him, who could be a companion in his search for game and adventure. He didn't dare hope he might be given a wolf—that would be asking for too much. A raven, perhaps, mused Korigan, though on second thought he wasn't sure how kindly Starhawk would take to sharing her roost with another bird.

At last Spartish tugged the last quill from the puppy's muzzle. He rubbed on a bit of ointment and sent her on her way with a gentle pat. Finally the beast master stood up and turned his attention to the waiting students.

"In Sanderstone, every young wizard must learn to work with a familiar," Spartish said sternly. "Familiars are your companions and helpers. They can become your friends, but do not make the mistake of thinking that they are humans in fur coats. A fox will always be a fox. Remember that. Respect it. You must learn to understand a creature who is very different from you, and find a way to work together. Are there any questions?"

Seven heads shook vigorously. The students were too eager to meet their familiars to waste time talking. Spartish smiled a little, as if he understood.

"Your teachers have taught you how to work with a familiar," he said, and his voice was milder now. "You should be able to communicate with yours at once. All of your other classes have been suspended for the day so that you may begin to learn your animal's ways. Once you have been assigned your familiar, you may leave."

Spartish walked over to his worktable and picked up a sheet of parchment. "Rixolar, son of Gorn," he called out.

A tall, blond boy leaped to his feet. Rixolar was from a family of battle wizards, and he looked the part of a young warrior. At fourteen, he was as tall and broad as most men, and as skilled with a sword as any man in the village. Rix was also the most dedicated student in the class, but with all this he still managed to find time to make Korigan's life miserable. Rix teased Korigan at every opportunity, insisting that the redheaded boy must be part forest elf. Sometimes Korigan wished there were some truth in Rix's taunts, for that would at least explain why he wasn't like anyone else in Sanderstone. Korigan was shorter than the other boys in his class, and he was as thin and wiry as an elf. He could see farther, run longer, and shoot better than anyone in the village. And he certainly wasn't much of a wizard!

Korigan watched with envy as Spartish called a large gray wolf from the shadows. "Kneel down, and extend your hand," the old man instructed Rix. "Let the wolf get your scent before you try to speak to him mind-to-mind. Remember, a familiar is first and foremost an animal. In this case, a wild animal."

With slow, cautious movements, Rix did as he was told. Korigan could almost smell the boy's fear, and he was sure that the wolf could! Yet the wolf came close and sniffed at Rix's knuckles. After a moment, the wolf wagged his tail, looking for a moment like nothing more than a big, gray dog. Rix's face relaxed and he rose to his feet. He left the room with a broad, triumphant grin on his lips and a wolf at his heels.

"Aileen, daughter of Tamar," Spartish called. He matched the girl with a young raccoon who had an impish, masked face and paws like clever little hands. Aileen laughed with delight and scampered off, her new companion-in-mischief gamboling close behind.

Two by two, the students and their new familiars left the room, until at last only Korigan was left. Before Spartish could call his name, the boy was on his feet. His heart pounded with excitement.

After a moment of tense silence, a large, yellow tabby cat stalked out from behind a bale of hay. It walked over to Korigan, looked the boy over from head to foot, and then sat down on its haunches and yawned widely.

Korigan gazed down at the tabby in disbelief. Surely, *this* could not be his familiar! He didn't even *like* cats! They were too cozy, too comfortable, too domesticated. They were lap-warmers, not real animals. And as for hunting, this cat looked too fat and lazy to catch its own tail!

The cat didn't seem too impressed with Korigan, either. It glared balefully at the dismayed boy, then lifted its hind leg and began to wash. Korigan knew enough about cats to know he'd just been insulted. He turned to Spartish, who had seated himself at his worktable. The old man was fussing with some thin strips of leather and paying no attention to the boy.

"A cat? Isn't there some mistake?" Korigan demanded.

Spartish squinted at the tabby. "No, no mistake," he muttered absently. "It's definitely a cat."

Korigan's words of protest were drowned out by a loud knock at the door of the Bestiary. Agtar, a tall, thin man with a pointed black beard and a haughty manner, swept into the

Bestiary without waiting for an invitation. Agtar was the secretary to Brucel, the headmaster of the School of Magic, and he always seemed very impressed with himself and his high position. With a flourish, the secretary handed a bit of paper to Spartish, as if he were presenting a royal edict. Which, in a way, he was. Magic was the most important thing in Sanderstone, and Brucel was the most powerful wizard in the village. He was also Korigan's uncle, a fact that did nothing to lessen the teasing Korigan received from his classmates.

Spartish glanced at the paper, and his face turned grim. "You're wanted in the headmaster's office at once, lad," he told Korigan. The boy reluctantly followed Agtar to the door. "Take your familiar with you!" the teacher called after him.

Korigan sent the cat a mental order, as he had been taught. The tabby yawned, curling its tiny pink tongue. Korigan tried again. The cat ignored him. The boy's cheeks flamed as he snatched up the cat and tucked it under his arm. He marched from the room, feeling the master's eyes on his back as keenly as if they had been daggers.

"Wait, Korigan."

The boy froze at the unexpected sound. Never once had Spartish called him by name. He turned to face the beast master, and the sympathy on the old man's face startled him. As Korigan looked into the master's understanding eyes, he thought he knew how Spartish's animals must feel.

"A cat's the only familiar for you. I'd hoped it might be otherwise, but as things stand, if you choose to be a wizard, you'll need a cat."

Korigan's brow furrowed in puzzlement. Of course he'd be a wizard. In Sanderstone, what else was there to be?

The old man rose and walked over to his student. He handed Korigan the leather straps. "These are new jesses for Starhawk," he said quietly. For a moment it seemed that he wanted to say more, then he nodded toward Agtar, who stood in the doorway, scowling and puffing indignantly at the delay. "That one's so full of himself he's nigh to bursting. You'd best be going."

Korigan hoisted the squirming, complaining cat onto his shoulder and followed Agtar. The secretary set a brisk pace through the winding streets toward Brucel's office. Sanderstone's streets were laid out like a dart board

17

in ever-widening circles, and the circles were connected at odd places by short alleys. The arrangement baffled the occasional visitor to Sanderstone, but every villager knew that the smaller the circle, the more important the location. At the very center of the village stood the Headmaster's Tower.

Each headmaster raised up his own tower through the power of magic. Brucel's tower was odd, even for Sanderstone. It looked like a giant, sprawling oak tree, crowned with leaves that never died even in the depth of winter. The leaves changed color with the seasons, however, and a few orange and crimson leaves floated about in the still morning air. They disappeared into mist before they touched the ground, and new leaves immediately appeared on the tree's branches.

Agtar slipped through the invisible door in the huge tree trunk, and up the steep, winding stair that led to Brucel's office. As Korigan followed, the cat finally managed to wriggle free. The tabby gave one last, indignant meow, and then pushed past Korigan to pad up the stairs.

It was said in Sanderstone that the treasures of a headmaster's tower could rival a

dragon's hoard. Shelves lined the walls of
Brucel's office, and each was crammed with
spellbooks bound in rare leathers and adorned
with jewels. Wondrous statues carved from
polished wood or green-veined marble stood
on pedestals, and candles in sconces of silver
and gold set the whole room a-sparkle. In the
center of this splendor stood Brucel, a dark,
bearded man clad in black silk robes embroidered with mystic symbols of power. With him
was Nim, apprentice to Thomas the Healer.
Nim's sandy brown whiskers and doleful expression gave him a remarkable resemblance
to his master, but that was only to be expected. In Sanderstone, where magical talent
was almost always inherited, an apprentice
was usually a close relative of his or her
master.

"Sit down, Korigan," Brucel said in a voice
as deep as a forest shadow. Korigan envied
his uncle that voice. His own voice tended to
crack at odd moments, leaping unexpectedly
skyward like a swallow in an updraft.

Korigan perched on the edge of a carved
wooden chair and tried to ignore the tabby
cat, who was sniffing purposefully at a potted
plant. "Thomas sends word from your mother,"

the headmaster said. "Maura is ill, and calling for you."

If Brucel felt concern for Maura, his younger sister, it hardly showed in his calm, resonant tones. But Korigan felt as if he'd been kicked in the stomach. No news could have been more unexpected. His mother, sick? Maura was the gayest, happiest, most *alive* person in Sanderstone. Hardly realizing he was doing so, Korigan shook his head in disbelief.

"It's true," Nim asserted. "Maura is very ill indeed. A fever set in, oh, about three days ago. It should have broken long before now. Master Thomas has done everything and more, but still Maura's condition does not improve," the apprentice said, sounding more than a little put out by the woman's lack of cooperation.

Three days? Korigan rose to his feet, shaking with rage and fear. "Why was I not told before this?" he demanded.

"Until recently, Maura's illness was not severe. We did not think it wise to *further* disrupt your studies," the headmaster said sternly, in a tone meant to remind Korigan that he was not exactly an attentive student. "But now this fever, and in her weakened state . . ." His voice trailed off, and he cleared his throat. "You should go to her at once."

Korigan bolted from the room and hurtled down the stairs. He heard his uncle calling after him, but he was too angry to answer and too worried to stop.

They should have told him! He'd had no word from his mother for ten days, and he cursed himself for not wondering why. Now fear sped through him as he raced through Sanderstone's streets toward the outermost circle of the village.

Near the forest's edge stood a small, vine-covered stone cottage that looked as if it had grown from the soil. For once, Korigan sprinted up the walk without pausing to inhale the scent of flowers and herbs that encircled the house like an embrace. He flung open the door and burst into the main room.

At first everything seemed as it should be. Bunches of drying herbs hung from the rafters. On a long wooden table stood neat rows of bottles holding herbal potions. The cottage was warm, fragrant, peaceful. It was also far too quiet: Maura usually sang as she worked with her flowers and herbs.

"Take ease, Maura; your son is here at last."

The unexpected sound of Brucel's voice made Korigan jump. The headmaster brushed aside the curtain that separated Maura's bedchamber from the main room. He stepped out, the tabby cat tucked under his arm.

"Your familiar," Brucel said pointedly as he set the cat down on a chair. "You apparently forgot that you must take the cat everywhere with you during your apprenticeship. You *also* forgot that I could magically transport all of us, instantly, to any place in Sanderstone."

The boy's face burned with shame. He didn't care about the cat, but Brucel was right about the other matter. Korigan's impulsive flight from the tower had wasted precious time. He brushed past the wizard and stepped into Maura's room. Dimly he took notice of the fire blazing in the fireplace, and of Thomas the Healer's grim face. Korigan stepped closer to the bed and looked down at his mother. A cry of dismay burst from him.

Everyone agreed that Maura the Herbalist was the most beautiful woman in the village, even if she was a bit odd. Her hair was the same bright red hue as her son's, and though it was long and thick she refused to bind it as a proper matron should. Her eyes were as blue as pansies, and roses bloomed year-round on her delicate face. She laughed easily, and sang often. Seeing her now, pale and still and silent, shook Korigan deeply.

Korigan sank to his knees and took one of his mother's hands between his own. It was as thin and weightless as a starved sparrow. He noted the sharp line of his mother's cheekbones, the dark hollows beneath her eyes. Her white face was hot and damp. She seemed almost lost beneath a pile of quilts, yet her thin form shook with a violent chill. Korigan knew without being told that her illness was grave.

As if through a haze, Korigan heard Brucel and the healer confer about Maura's treatment. "Only the most powerful of potions can restore her now," Thomas said softly. "Alas, we haven't anything strong enough in Sanderstone."

"Name what you need, and you will have it," the headmaster vowed.

The healer hesitated. "The only remedy that will aid us now is the horn of a unicorn. Now, I don't like this any better than you do, Brucel, but—"

"No!"

Brucel spoke softly, but with such force that Thomas fell back a step. The healer quickly recovered his composure, and even went so far as to shake a finger in the wizard's face. "This is no time to discuss ancient legends! The time when men spoke with unicorns is long past, and all the wishing in the world won't bring it back. Modern magic—*that's* what is needed to restore Maura to health. Granted, potions made from unicorns' horns are terribly expensive—"

"Do you think I care about the expense?" Brucel demanded. "But think, man. Such potions can be ordered, but how long would that take?"

"Three, maybe four months," Thomas admitted.

"And does Maura have that much time?"

The healer's silence answered the question all too clearly. After several tense moments, Thomas cleared his throat. "We do not have to order the potion. I know how to concoct one, but I must have the proper ingredients. No, listen to me," Thomas said, cutting short the headmaster's next argument. "If you value your sister's life, you must find someone to hunt down a unicorn and kill it. Soon," Thomas added in a grim tone, as he glanced toward the sick woman's bed.

"There must be another way," Brucel said, but there was little conviction in his voice.

"If there is, I know it not. You know as well as I that a unicorn's horn is used only as a last resort. Yet, it often succeeds where all else fails."

"But you're speaking of a magical beast, against which no wizard's magic can prevail!"

"Send a hunter, then."

"Sanderstone is a community of wizards; no one here is a skilled hunter," Brucel argued. "A unicorn is nearly impossible to track, and even harder to bring down."

"*I can do it.*"

The two men fell silent, and suddenly Korigan realized that he had spoken the words aloud. The boy repeated his claim, this time with more conviction.

"He *is* the best shot in the village," Thomas said, eyeing Korigan as if seeing him for the first time.

Brucel started to protest, but the healer nodded pointedly toward Korigan's mother. The headmaster's lips folded into a tight line, and he nodded, once.

"It's settled then," Thomas said. "You'd best get the boy on his way at once."

Maura stirred, and her pale lips struggled to form words. The effort sent her into a fit of coughing, and her frail body shook like a storm-tossed willow. Thomas was at her side in a heartbeat.

"Don't try to speak," the healer admonished her. As soon as the racking cough subsided, he held a cup to Maura's lips and tipped some amber liquid into her mouth. Maura lay still against the pillows, but her fever-bright eyes pleaded with her son.

The boy took her hand again and gave it a gentle squeeze. "Don't worry, Mother. I'll be back soon, and then you'll get better. I promise you this."

Once again she tried to speak, but Thomas's medicine pulled her relentlessly toward slumber. When her eyes fluttered shut, Korigan kissed her on the forehead and quietly left the room.

As he hurried back toward his quarters to prepare for the hunt, it occurred to him that, at long last, he was leaving Sanderstone. Korigan had dreamed about this moment for years, but never had he imagined a quest as grand as the one before him. A unicorn hunt was a wondrous adventure. He might not be much of a wizard, but he was a fine hunter. When he brought back the unicorn's horn, he would prove his worth to all of Sanderstone!

Korigan knew he should be elated. Yet as he jogged toward the School of Magic, all he could think about was the deep sadness in his mother's eyes.

2

Percival

Korigan and his classmates lived in a small wooden building that stood not far from the Bestiary, just across the street from the village stables. He made way to his room with breathless haste, and in a few minutes more he'd gathered the things he would need for the trip: clothing, a warm cloak, and his bow. He filled his quiver with arrows and slid the strap over his shoulder. Thus supplied, he hurried across the street to collect his horse and his hawk.

Bronwyn nickered softly as Korigan entered

the stall, tossing her russet head in welcome. Despite his hurry, the boy smiled and scratched the patch of white between the mare's eyes. "I'm glad to see you, too," Korigan whispered, and leaned his head against his friend's velvety neck.

A rustle of wings drew Korigan's eyes to a ledge at the back of the stall. He stepped away from the mare and pulled a long, cuffed leather gauntlet from his belt. He thrust his left hand into the glove, made a fist and extended his arm before him, elbow bent. "Come, lady hawk," he called softly.

With a delicate flutter, a peregrin falcon swept out of the shadows and landed on Korigan's forearm. Yellow eyes met his, and the hawk's head tilted at an inquisitive angle.

"We're going hunting, Starhawk," Korigan said. For the first time, a bit of excitement crept into his voice. Any time spent with hawk and horse was usually stolen from his studies, and their hunts were never long enough to satisfy him. Now days and nights of adventure lay before them, untainted by magic's never-ending demands. "Just you, me, and Bronwyn," Korigan said with deep satisfaction.

"Think again," suggested a dour male voice behind him.

Korigan whirled, looking this way and that for the speaker. To his eyes, he was alone in the stables. Starhawk's golden eyes saw differently, and she shrieked with fierce rage. Her wings bated wildly, and sharp talons tensed around Korigan's arm as she prepared to take flight.

Speaking soothingly, Korigan raised his ungloved hand to stroke the falcon. Starhawk nipped him sharply. With a cry of surprise and pain, Korigan jerked back his hand. The falcon flew to her perch on the ledge. From the safety of her dark corner, she shrieked and scolded.

The straw at his feet rustled, and Korigan looked down. There was the fat yellow tabby, gingerly testing each step as if the straw scratched its delicate paws. Ignoring both hawk and boy, the tabby leaped onto a low barrel and began to wash.

The boy's first impulse was to shoo the cat away. Yet Starhawk was out of harm's reach and beginning to quiet down. And, whether Korigan liked it or not, the cat was his familiar and it was supposed to go wherever he went.

"Don't worry, Starhawk," he spoke soothingly. "That cat can't bother you. See how fat and lazy it is. It probably can't jump any higher than that barrel."

"*It?* Excuse me, but did you say *it*?"

The words were spoken in a deeply offended tone. Once again Korigan whirled about, but there was no one else in the stall. He took a long, steadying breath and wondered whether this might be another of Aileen's pranks.

"My *name* is Percival," the plaintive voice announced, "and I'm over here."

Slowly, Korigan's gaze shifted toward the sound. The yellow tabby perched on the barrel, regarding him with unblinking gold-green eyes. "Percival—my name," the cat repeated with exaggerated patience. His small pink mouth worked as he spoke the words in a voice as clear and deep as a man's. "Not that you've asked, of course."

"You can talk!" Korigan blurted.

"Of course. All cats *can* talk. We just don't want to."

Korigan's head bobbed in dazed agreement. He'd always suspected as much. "Then why—"

"It's sadly obvious, I should think. Wizards can communicate mind-to-mind with their familiars. *Wizards*," Percival repeated with scathing emphasis. His tail switched in exasperation. "Do you think I'm happy about this? Human speech is undignified, not at all suited for creatures of grace and subtlety. But what else am I to do? Outfit you with a tail and whiskers and train you to speak feline?"

Korigan settled back on his heels and considered that notion with interest. "Cats have a language," he mused. "And I could learn to speak it?"

"Hmmph! Not if you had nine lives," Percival said flatly. "I see you're no better with sarcasm than you are with mental speech." The cat sat back on his haunches and examined a newly washed forepaw. "So. It's plain you're not much of a wizard. What *can* you do?"

Korigan folded his arms. "I hunt," he said shortly.

The cat's eyes widened. "Really. That's the best news I've heard all day. See if you can scare me up a couple of mice, there's a good lad."

Grinding his teeth to hold back an angry retort, Korigan turned and picked up the mare's harness. The wonder of a talking familiar had faded, and he had no intention of taking orders from a tabby cat. "You see to your hunting, puss, and I'll see to mine," he said shortly.

"Ah, yes. The unicorn hunt." Percival's tongue flicked out in an unmistakable gesture of distaste. "That reminds me—you will need to get supplies and stop by the Headmaster's Tower before we leave."

Korigan's jaw dropped. A wizard apprentice had to keep his familiar with him at all times; that was the rule in Sanderstone. Korigan knew all about that. It had never occurred to him, however, that the rules of Sanderstone would follow him into the forest.

"Before *we* leave?" he asked, hoping there might be some mistake.

"We," the cat repeated grimly. "Do you think I'm happy about this? And if you think I'm walking on this fool's errand, you'd better think twice. Use a pillion saddle, so that I can ride behind you."

That was simply too much for Korigan. He remembered every oath he'd ever heard, and he used them, loudly. Oh, he could just imagine Rixolar's taunts: Sir Korigan, the noble knight, riding forth with a tabby cat instead of a princess!

But what else was he to do? He was bound by the rules of his apprenticeship. So Korigan found the long, padded saddle made for two riders and strapped it on Bronwyn's back. That done, he snatched up a pair of saddlebags to hold his provisions. He was about to storm out of the stables, when something else occurred to him.

"You'd better come with me," he said grudgingly to the cat. "I don't trust you here alone with Starhawk."

"If you're referring to that poor excuse for a chicken up there, you've got no quarrel with me. Falcons are useless—too thin to eat, too mean to chase. But yes, I'm definitely coming with you. I wouldn't miss this for a cowful of cream," Percival said in a smug voice. He hopped down from his perch and ambled along behind Korigan, who was still too angry to be curious about the cat's odd choice of words.

In minutes they reached the center of the village. Near the Headmaster's Tower stood a semicircle of shops and warehouses that supplied Sanderstone with day-to-day necessities, exotic goods from far markets, and a vast array of spell components. With Percival close on his heels, Korigan hurried toward Peg the Provisioner's shop. Peg was a hearth mage, skilled in such small magics as tending fires, growing yeasts, and brewing ale and mead.

Korigan pushed open the heavy wooden door. The shop was a cozy place, lined with well-stocked shelves and crowded with barrels. They were greeted by a pleasant jumble of scents, and by Peg herself. Korigan absently returned the shopkeeper's cheery welcome. His eyes roved the shelves as he mentally selected what he would need: dried fruit, nuts, a few medicines and bandages, some dried fish and meat in case the hunting was not good, an extra water flask.

As he selected his provisions, Korigan heard the chirp of a cricket from some hidden corner of the shop. When cold weather approached, crickets often came indoors in search of food and warmth. On other days such as this, when Korigan was snug in his mother's cottage by the woods, the chirping of a hearthside cricket sounded like a cheery lullaby. Now, with a journey before him, the cricket's song spoke to him of long autumn nights.

"I'll need another travel blanket," Korigan

said as he piled his purchases on the counter. "The crickets are singing early this year. Cold weather's just around the turn."

Peg scowled. "I've been trying to catch that fool cricket all the day long," she complained. "I keep a clean place and can't be bothered with bugs." Her eyes fell on Percival and narrowed with speculation. "Say, you don't suppose your cat could hunt it down?"

The cat shot Korigan a glare of such wounded dignity that, despite himself, Korigan grinned. "The cricket's well enough where he is. We're in his forest, after all."

"That we're not," Peg said emphatically. "Sanderstone is a civilized town."

Korigan sighed. He was always amazed at how estranged the villagers were from the land they lived on and the forest that surrounded them. If Sanderstone were magically moved to a cloud bank or dropped into the sea, few people in the village would notice much of a difference.

"Civilized or not, Sanderstone is in the middle of the forest, and there are insects in the forest," Korigan pointed out.

"Well, I don't see why there *have* to be!" Peg retorted.

Korigan thought of termites changing fallen logs to dust, pollen-dusted bees whizzing about, worms tunneling dead leaves into loam. But what was any of that to Sanderstone? So Korigan pointed out, "Bugs can be useful as spell components."

"That's true enough," Peg allowed. "Doesn't mean I have to like them here in my store, though."

With another sigh, Korigan gathered up his purchases. Peg added a second, larger bundle to his load. "This goes to Headmaster Brucel. He was in earlier and settled up your account as well as his own. Off with you, now!"

By tradition, no one left Sanderstone without first asking the headmaster's blessing, so Korigan and Percival ran across the street to the oak-tree tower.

Brucel was waiting for them at the base of tree. The wizard was dressed in plain, sturdy clothes of russet and brown, and shod in high leather boots. A heavy brown cloak hung about his shoulders. There was a dagger in his belt, and he carried a staff of dark oak, elaborately carved with runes Korigan had never bothered to learn.

A dismayed but enlightened Korigan stared

at his uncle. Brucel intended to come on the hunt! On *his* hunt!

The headmaster raised a questioning eyebrow. "Surely you did not think to go alone?"

Korigan's cheeks flamed with embarrassment, but he kept his head high and met his uncle's eyes. With a touch of surprise, Korigan noted that Brucel was not much taller than he was. The wizard looked much less imposing without the magnificent embroidered robes that proclaimed his office.

"One person can track, where two might frighten away the quarry," Korigan said sturdily. "I know the forest; I can walk silently even among the fallen leaves. With all respect, Uncle, a man unskilled in the ways of the woods would be more hindrance than help to me."

The wizard let this comment pass. "And do you know where a unicorn might be found?"

Korigan's gaze dropped. He had not thought that far ahead. "I can track anything in the forest," he said stubbornly.

"It might be that you can. But the unicorn's glade lies past the forest you know, three days' travel and more. You could wander a lifetime without finding a unicorn's trail."

"Then give me a map," Korigan pleaded. "I can follow it to the glade."

"Could you also see the shifting magic that hides the unicorn's glade from common sight?" the wizard demanded.

Once again, it came down to magic! Korigan admitted defeat with a shrug.

Brucel glanced down at Percival, who had been listening to this exchange with an expression of smug interest on his furry, yellow face. "You will need to use a pillion saddle for your familiar," the wizard informed his nephew.

"So I have been told," Korigan said through stiff lips.

* * * * *

The one thing Korigan would not budge on was Starhawk. Where he went, so did the falcon. Brucel gave in with the detached air of one who has greater matters to consider, and then busied himself saddling a sturdy gray mare.

At last they were on their way. Percival, of course, was seated behind Korigan on the padded pillion saddle, and Starhawk perched uneasily on the pommel in front.

Starhawk was still more wild than tame, and Korigan wouldn't have it any other way. Unlike most falconers, Korigan refused to put a hood on his hawk. Nor would he tie her to the pommel; the new jesses that Spartish had given Korigan were still in his bag. The boy wanted Starhawk free, so that she could fight or fly if Percival's hunting instincts ever surfaced.

The small band rode in silence to the edge of the village. Korigan's eyes lingered on his mother's vine-covered stone cottage and its wonderful gardens, and a lump rose in his throat. He swallowed hard and fixed his thoughts on the journey ahead.

Korigan turned to Brucel, who had wrapped himself in his cloak as if to shut out the world. "What course will we take?" Korigan asked.

The wizard aroused himself from his reverie. "North, toward the moors."

A shiver of excitement raced up Korigan's spine. He'd often dreamed of traveling the moorland, and there was no better time to do so than these last warm days of autumn. With the coming of winter, ducks headed for warmer climes. The shallow marshes would be alive with waterfowl, and he and Starhawk would have fine hunting along the way.

They followed the main road until it came to a broad, shallow river. A wooden bridge spanned the water, and just before the bridge a path branched off toward the north. This path was narrow, and trees met overhead in a canopy of scarlet and orange. Korigan reined Bronwyn northward, and, with a sigh of deep satisfaction, he settled in for a long ride.

Not many minutes had passed, however, before Korigan noticed that something was very wrong. The forest around them was far too quiet. Even the trees overhead seemed watchful. No birds twittered in their branches, no squirrels scolded the passing riders. The boy glanced over at Brucel, but the wizard seemed deep in his own thoughts and completely unaware of his surroundings.

And that, Korigan decided, was fine with him. This was *his* hunt, and even though he couldn't keep Brucel from tagging alone, *he* could do whatever needed to be done along the way. The boy removed his bow from its shoulder strap and placed it across his lap, an arrow at the ready. He watched and listened for any sign of danger.

Within minutes his keen ears heard a faint click. The sound came from a thick stand of vine-draped sumac a little way up the path. Korigan's heart thumped as he recognized the sound. Most people, if they'd heard the click at all, would have thought it was the call of an insect or the sound of an acorn dropping onto the rocky ground. But Korigan knew the sound of someone setting a crossbow when he heard it.

From the corner of his eye he peered deeply into the bushes. At least two dark forms crouched in the shadows, and a stray bit of sunlight glinted off a ready arrow.

Korigan's fingers tightened around his bow, but his mind whirled with indecision. When hunting, he never shot unless he was sure of a clean hit. This was no animal, but an armed enemy who had the advantage of strength and number. Yet Korigan had never raised a weapon against a man. He wasn't sure he could.

He had but a minute to decide, for he and Brucel rode steadily toward certain ambush. They passed an ancient oak, and the thick trunk gave them a moment's safety, shielding them from harm and from sight. Korigan nocked his arrow and raised the bow to his shoulder. Remembering the location of that glint of light, he pictured the archer in his mind and aimed for the hand that would hold the arrow ready. As soon as Bronwyn cleared the oak, Korigan drew a deep breath and fired. As his arrow streaked toward the bushes, Korigan held his breath and hoped with all his heart that he had guessed the archer's position aright.

A loud oath shattered the silence of the forest. Korigan had a second arrow ready before the shout of pain died away. Leaves rustled wildly as two rough-looking men rushed toward the path, daggers drawn. They pulled up short at the sight of the grim young archer.

A third man stepped onto the path, clasping his right arm. Korigan's arrow had found its mark. Despite his pain-twisted face, this man had an air of command about him, and his clothes, though worn and travel-stained, looked like some sort of uniform. His eyes darted from Korigan to Brucel, as if he were trying to decide who was in charge. Although the boy was armed, the wounded man addressed himself to the wizard.

"Where are they?" he demanded. "Where

are the other travelers?"

Brucel met the man's gaze calmly. The wizard held out both hands, palms up, as if to show that he had no weapons. "The boy and I travel alone."

"Do I look like a fool?" the man shouted. "We've been following you people for days! The others must be nearby, and it'll go easier on you if you tell us where they are."

"You are mistaken," the wizard said in the same even tone.

"I doubt it." The man turned a menacing frown upon his men. "Get them. The boy can only shoot one of you!"

The men exchanged dismayed glances. It was clear that neither of them wanted that particular honor. Marking their hesitation, Korigan drew back the arrow and sighted down the leader. For a long moment, no one moved. No one even breathed.

"Don't, boy," Brucel said softly. "Save your arrows for more important matters. These men are no threat to us."

Korigan shot a look of pure disbelief at the wizard, but he did not lower his weapon.

"I said, put that down," Brucel said, this time more sharply. "Look at them!"

The boy turned his gaze back to the ruffians. The three men stood so still they might as well have been statues. Korigan remembered the way Brucel had held out his hands, and his shoulders slumped as he realized what had happened. The wizard's gesture was part of a simple spell, one that Korigan should have learned last summer but never quite got around to mastering. Thanks to Brucel's magic, the men had been magically frozen. They would stay that way until the next day dawned.

Magic, Korigan fumed. Always magic! All his skill with the bow, all his knowledge of the forest could not compare to the simplest of spells. In sheer frustration, Korigan pointed his arrow toward the sky and let it fly. He watched it disappear into the trees, and with it went all his illusions about his own importance on this quest.

But Brucel was not content to let the matter rest. "You could have killed that man," he said sternly.

"But I did not," Korigan protested. "I hit exactly what I aimed for."

"Perhaps so, but from now on, you are not to take matters into your own hands. There

are better ways of dealing with such distur-
bances, as you have seen. Now, let's move on
as quickly as we can. The river crosses this
path again a few miles ahead, in a grassy
clearing. We will make camp there."

The wizard slapped his reins against the
gray mare's neck, and the horse took off at a
gentle trot. Korigan gritted his teeth and
urged Bronwyn to keep pace. Behind him,
Percival—who had been mercifully silent during most of the trip—began to purr in short,
loud bursts. Korigan didn't have to read his
familiar's thoughts to know that the cat was
laughing at him.

3
The Travelers

For the remainder of the day, Korigan and Brucel rode along in a silence broken only by the sound of the nearby river gurgling over the shallows, and by an occasional cranky meow from Percival. Although Korigan found it fairly easy to ignore the cat, he could not dismiss from his mind the encounter with the ruffians. Who were those men, and whom were they seeking?

Until now, Korigan had not bothered to look for tracks, for the trade road was well traveled. He kept a close watch now, yet he had seen no sign that anyone else had passed this way. And if there were signs to see, Korigan was confident that he would have found them. As he pondered the matter, a possible answer came to him. He decided to test his theory when they got to Brucel's clearing.

When they finally arrived at their intended campsite, the sky was stained with the purple and silver of an autumn sunset. Brucel called a halt, and Korigan swung down from Bronwyn's back. Percival stretched, yawned, and waited pointedly to be lifted down from his pillion. Korigan absently swatted the cat down from his perch. Percival hissed once and then took off into the bushes on business of his own, emitting feline grumbles as he went. Brucel tended the horses and then headed off toward the river. Starhawk took to the sky, as if to stretch her wings before darkness fell. Under the guise of collecting firewood, Korigan searched the riverbank.

As he suspected, there were tracks—spots of damp grass and ribbons of faint moisture—coming up the bank from the river. Korigan figured that there were about a dozen small wagons in the mysterious group, and perhaps twice that many horses.

This discovery puzzled him. Merchant caravans would take the trade route, for this northern road led only into the wilderness. Whatever their purpose, these travelers had come through recently. The day was cool and the clearing well shaded, but even so the tracks would dry out quickly. The group clearly knew they were pursued, and they had cleverly evaded the ruffians. Korigan figured that they must have taken to the river at the point where the north road branched off from the trade route, just before the bridge. The river was shallow, and it could hide both their tracks and the sounds of their passing. But who were they, and why did they run?

Korigan had only so much time to devote to the mystery, for he wanted to hunt with Starhawk before the light faded. Falcons did not hunt in the dark, and tonight a successful hunt meant more than dinner to Korigan. The wizard's presence made Korigan feel useless and small, and the young hunter was determined to do whatever he could to contribute to their quest.

Yet the night approached swiftly, and he knew that soon Starhawk would have to find a perch. Korigan was about to call off the evening's hunt when a nearby clump of tall grasses rustled wildly.

Two quail burst into startled flight. In the opposite direction ran Percival, his green eyes wild as he streaked toward the safety of the campfire. The sight was amusing, but Korigan had no smile to spare for the frantic tabby. The boy's attention was fixed on the sunset sky where Starhawk wheeled and circled in the dying light.

The falcon folded her wings and dropped into a dive. Fast as an arrow, she hurtled toward the nearest quail. At the last moment her wings opened and her talons flexed. She snatched the quail out of the air and then wheeled sharply into a sweeping descent. The hawk dipped low into the clearing and dropped the quail near Korigan.

Her wings beat steadily as she climbed into the sky once again. Starhawk did not waste time climbing for another diving swoop, but closed quickly on the much slower quail. The falcon's path led her under her intended prey. Agile and deadly, the falcon rolled in midair, caught the bird in her talons, and rolled upright in one smooth movement. The triumphant Starhawk circled down to her human friend and laid her second prize at his feet.

Pride and excitement coursed through Korigan. Starhawk had been hunting for most of the summer, but she was just now learning to share. This was the first time she had brought her kill to Korigan and waited patiently for her portion. As he prepared the quail, he praised the falcon with soft words and fed her choice bits of the meat.

Meanwhile, Percival had kneaded Korigan's travel blanket into a comfortable fireside bed. He glared at the boy and his falcon. "By all the fuss you're making, you'd think the hawk had caught those quail without any aid," the cat complained.

Korigan paused in his work to shoot an inquisitive glance toward the tabby. "I found the quail, you know, and I flushed them out of hiding," Percival said in a haughty tone. "That leaves some debate as to who is the better hunter."

Korigan was sorely tempted to remind the cat of his flight from the bushes, but he swallowed his taunts. It occurred to him that Percival's pompous dignity, though annoying, was shared by every other cat Korigan had ever known. He could not fault the tabby for acting according to his nature. Nor was it Percival's fault that he was more suited to the fireside than the forest. Korigan well knew the sting caused by cruel or careless words, and he would not remind Percival of his deficiencies.

"Come then, and claim the hunter's portion," the boy said gravely.

The cat shot an uneasy look at Starhawk, who was tearing at her dinner with that deadly beak. "If it's all the same to you, I prefer to dine alone," Percival said grandly. "And cook it first, if you please. Raw quail doesn't agree with me."

Again stifling a smile, Korigan set to work. Soon the quails were sizzling on a spit over the fire. When the meat was ready, he cut a generous portion for Percival and then set off to look for his uncle.

He found the wizard near the river, seated on a rock. To Korigan's surprise, Brucel was playing a musical instrument. The wizard's fingers danced in jerky movements over the sound holes of a small wooden pipe, but no sound emerged. Most likely Brucel had cast a sphere of silence, Korigan guessed, so that he might play in privacy. The boy winced as he recognized the instrument, and he silently blessed his uncle for casting such a thoughtful spell. For Brucel held a shawm, an instrument that, when played well, was barely tolerable. At best, it sounded like a duck with a head cold. Korigan took a deep breath and waded into the sphere of silence.

Immediately he wished he hadn't. In Brucel's hands, the shawm squalled and shrilled in agonized protest. Korigan cleared his throat, loudly.

Startled, Brucel looked up. A sheepish expression crept across the wizard's face. When Korigan announced that supper was ready, the wizard tucked the instrument into his travel bag and, without a word, followed Korigan back to the campfire. Somehow, Korigan knew better than to comment on the wizard's music.

As they ate, Korigan told his uncle about the tracks he had found. He described the size of the group of travelers and explained how they had evaded the ruffians. Brucel nodded thoughtfully as he listened.

"I understand the bandit's words—when he asked about the other *travelers*—better now," the wizard said. "You may have heard of a people who wander about the land, going wherever pleases them. They call themselves Travelers. We will no doubt overtake them tomorrow, and they will welcome us into their camp. That is their way. But do not mention to any of them the purpose of our quest," he cautioned. "When asked, say only that we are gathering ingredients for medicines. That is true enough, and will suffice."

A people who made the road their home! Korigan was intrigued by such a notion, and he pressed his uncle for more information. But Brucel curtly reminded the boy that dawn came early.

So, after supper, Korigan banked the fire and rolled himself in his spare travel blanket. He was so excited he was certain he would not be able to sleep, but the long day of riding told. He drifted off to the lullaby of Percival's loud, rhythmic purring.

* * * * *

They were on their way again before first light, and they had not ridden far before they met the first of the Travelers. Without warning, a boy no older than Korigan stepped out onto the path before them. He smiled pleasantly, but his black eyes held an unmistakable challenge.

Korigan observed the boy with deep interest, for he was very different from anyone Korigan knew in Sanderstone. The Traveler's skin was bronzed by the sun and wind, and his long black hair was pulled back and tied with a leather thong. His eyes held an untamed gleam, like those of an inquisitive raven, and he studied the two riders with eyes that saw and measured.

The Traveler politely asked their business and accepted their explanation with a cheerful nod. He laughed delightedly when Korigan told what had befallen the ruffians. After giving his name as Rimko, he invited them to follow him to the camp. Perhaps, Korigan mused as he rode along, most people would see such acceptance as dangerously trusting. Rimko carried no visible weapons, but Korigan had the feeling that the young Traveler was not unarmed. He suspected that the Travelers could handle whatever challenge two riders could provide.

The Travelers' camp was well hidden in a forest glade. Brightly painted wooden caravans stood in a circle, and a fragrant breakfast of fruited porridge and fresh game cooked over a number of small fires. Each fire had been built on a patch of bare earth, where the sod had been carefully cut and peeled away. Korigan took note of this and nodded with approval. No doubt the sod would be replaced after the fires cooled, leaving little trace of the Travelers' passing. Korigan had never thought of such a thing, but he saw its merit. As his eyes darted about the camp, he realized that there was much he could learn here.

After Rimko had shown the newcomers around the camp, he took them to meet his mother, a thin, dark-eyed woman whom he proudly introduced as Queen of the Travelers. She listened intently as Rimko repeated what Brucel and Korigan had told him, though she interrupted him frequently with brief bursts of coughing.

Korigan noted that the queen's eyes were red-rimmed and her breathing scratchy—sure signs of the autumn-itch. Many in Sanderstone had this illness during the final days of harvest, and Korigan's mother was kept busy from late summer until the first frost brewing potions and simples. This memory reminded him painfully of Maura's illness, and of the gravity of his hunt. Yet, as eager as he was to be on his way, Korigan felt a strong pull to these itinerant people. So he listened closely when Rimko's mother painfully cleared her throat and began to speak.

"We have heard your story, and now we offer you ours," the queen said in a thin, ragged voice. "Several days past, in a place not too far from here, men took to arms. Every young man in the area was pressed into service. We had the misfortune to pass through during this time, and they would have taken Rimko to fight, though their quarrel was nothing to us."

"And that is not your way," reasoned Korigan.

"That is not Rimko's way," she corrected. "Had he wished to join the battle, he would have done so. But why would he fight in a land dispute between two fat and lazy lords? Fah!" she said, throwing up her hands in disgust. "As if a man, any man, could own the land he walks upon!

"When they tried to take him by force, Rimko challenged an officer to single combat and bested him. Defeated and shamed before his men, this officer made a vow of vengeance.

This was the man you met," she concluded grimly.

"We left him and his two men only a half day's travel behind," Brucel said.

The queen dismissed this news with a wave of her hand. "We are not so worried about those three. After we have eaten, we will leave. You are welcome to share our food, and our path as well."

"Thank you, but our business is urgent. We must move on as quickly as possible," Korigan said.

Brucel responded with a wry smile. "As for that, we will be hard pressed to keep pace with them," he told his nephew. Turning to the queen, he accepted her offers with thanks.

Rimko grinned happily and drew Korigan aside. "It is good that you will be with us," he said companionably. "I would like to learn more of your hunting falcon, and why you bring a village cat into the forest. You can tell me all about it while I show you a game we Travelers play."

He took Korigan to the edge of camp and pointed to a fallen tree. The young Traveler took several small knives from hidden pockets in his boots and from the sash he wore around his waist. He took a knife by the tip and pointed toward the log. "See that knothole, the one right under the branch?"

When Korigan nodded, Rimko flicked the knife toward the target. It disappeared into the knothole without touching the edges.

The Traveler handed another knife to Korigan. "Now you try."

Feeling a bit awkward, Korigan mimicked Rimko's movements as best he could. The knife tumbled end over end before falling into the dirt. Korigan grimaced, but Rimko clapped him heartily on the back.

"Everyone does so at first. You do better than most. Here—try again."

Korigan tried again and again, carefully following Rimko's cheery instructions. After ten throws, he managed to hit the log. Rimko burst into applause, but Korigan shook his head. He had his own measure of success. Again and again he threw, until at last the knife disappeared into the knothole. Even that was not enough. Korigan took up three more knives and sent them, one after another, into the small opening. None of them so much as touched the edges of the knothole. Korigan nodded with satisfaction.

Rimko gave a long, low whistle. "Never have I seen such a thing. How is it, that you learn so quickly and well?"

In response, Korigan took his bow from its shoulder strap and quickly fitted an arrow. He sent the arrow into the knothole, and then two more after it. There was a faint chink of metal on metal as each arrowhead glanced off the others. Korigan turned to the openmouthed Traveler.

"I hit what I aim at," he said simply. "Once I understood how the knife should be thrown, the rest came quickly."

"We are taught to hunt at an early age, yet none of us can shoot so well!" Rimko said in a tone of deep respect. "And never have we hunted with hawks. If such skills were taught to all town dwellers, even I might think about giving up the road!"

Korigan's heart warmed with his new friend's praise, but he was unaccustomed to having his skills valued, and he did not know how to respond. So he answered with an awkward shrug, then turned away to retrieve his arrows.

As he bent to tug them from the log, Korigan saw a way that he could repay the Travelers' kindness. In the shadow of the fallen tree grew a small plant with leaves of silvery green. Korigan plucked a leaf and crushed it in his fingers. It gave off a sharp, spicy scent that he knew well. He had often gathered the plant for his mother, who used it in several of her medicines but could not grow it in her gardens. "Some plants grow where they will, and not where you would have them," Maura had said. Within the walls of a garden, they lost much of their essence and soon faded. Korigan had always felt a kinship to this untamed plant. He carefully gathered a few of the leaves—taking no more than needed—and slipped them into one of the tiny linen bags that he always carried for such purposes.

After the communal breakfast, Korigan offered the herbs to Rimko's mother. "Crush these leaves, and steep them in a tea. Breathing the steam will clear your head, and drinking the tea will sooth the cough," he explained.

"I have heard of such things," the Queen said, "for many Travelers are well versed in herb lore, and rival the best herbalists and healers in the land. This little band, alas, has no healer of its own." With a rueful smile, she reached for Korigan's little bag. "I thank you for your kindness. Better the medicines of a town-dweller than none at all."

She loosened the drawstring and shook the bag over her open palm, evidently expecting a sprinkling of dried herbs. Her eyes widened when a single, silver-green leaf fell into her hand.

The Traveler fixed Korigan with a long, speculative gaze. "This herb was freshly gathered."

Korigan nodded. "It grows only in the wild."

"Ah. And how is it that you, a dweller in towns, know of such plants?" she asked.

"My mother is an herbalist. She knows plants better than I know my horse and falcon," the boy explained. "I was raised amid her gardens, and could not help but learn a bit about plants and their uses. Mother also told me about wild herbs, and where they might be found. Sometimes, when hunting, I would find a plant she described and bring it home. For several years now, I have gathered this herb for her, and others that will not grow in a garden."

"Then your mother knows the forest," the Queen mused. "Is she perhaps a Traveler, one of those who has settled?"

Korigan sat back on his heels as he considered this question. He knew that his mother was no Traveler, but how had she learned about wild plants if all her life had been lived in Sanderstone? He knew nothing of his father; it suddenly occurred to him that he understood his mother little better. So once again he answered with a shrug, and was grateful when the queen turned to other matters.

"My son has spoken of your skills. Yet perhaps there is more, something Rimko has not told me. We shall see." The queen looked long and searchingly into Korigan's eyes. Strangely, he did not feel uncomfortable with her scrutiny. Finally the Traveler nodded, satisfied.

"You do not belong among town dwellers," she said simply. "When your searching is over, there is a place for you among us, if ever you should want it."

She rose and left Korigan sitting openmouthed by the fire. Brucel drew near, and he eyed his nephew sharply.

"There are more roads to travel than you have seen," the wizard said softly. Korigan felt the weight of more than one meaning behind the words. He waited for Brucel to explain, but for several long moments the wizard sat in silence.

"That was well done," he said at last. "Bringing the queen those healing herbs was not only a kindness, but a clever ruse. The Travelers will assume we are in the forest to gather medicinal plants."

"Why don't we just tell them what we seek?" Korigan asked. "It might be that they have seen the unicorn, and have information that can help us on our hunt."

Brucel shook his head. "Tell no one of our purpose," he said sternly. "If these people knew what we hunted, they would drive us from the forest." The wizard rose and turned away, but Korigan's sharp ears caught the words Brucel murmured to himself as he walked away.

"They would drive us from the forest, and rightly so."

4
Goblin Country

All the next day, the band of Travelers made their way northward with astonishing speed. Rimko and Korigan rode together at the end of the caravan, talking and laughing as if they'd been lifelong friends. The young Traveler was fascinated by Starhawk, and Korigan was only too happy to show off the falcon's beauty and skill.

And so a joyously content Starhawk took to the sky. The hunting was good, but on such a day she would have been happy with flight alone. She swirled playfully through updrafts and bathed in the mist of the lowest clouds. The falcon's delight was enhanced by her awareness of Korigan's unusually happy mood.

For some time now, Starhawk had been able to sense the young human's thoughts. These came to her not in words, but in pictures and feelings. What she perceived most often from him was numb despair. To Starhawk, the reason for this was clear: Korigan lacked wings.

The falcon would happily share flight with him—she knew how. Again and again she'd asked him to join her, but so far her voice had gone unheard. This distressed the beautiful bird, for she loved Korigan with fierce devotion.

Ofttimes, when Korigan was trapped in his classrooms, the falcon had sought out the company of Sanderstone's beast master. Old Spartish had told her that most humans mewed their hawks, either caging them or placing leather hoods over their heads so they could not fly. Korigan had never confined her so. Since the day she had first learned flight, Starhawk had been free to come and go as she pleased. While Korigan spent his days list-

lessly studying the art of magic, Starhawk
flew. She always came back, and Korigan
regarded each return as the gift that it was.
Except for her grief over Korigan's strange
captivity, Starhawk was well content with her
life.

Yet as Korigan learned magic—almost
despite himself—Starhawk found herself
learning and changing, too. Her eyes were as
keen as ever in daylight, but recently she'd
found herself able to pierce the deepest shadows of the stables, even to fly out into the
night. For weeks now, Starhawk had vied
with perplexed owls for her share of night-
wandering game. Some days she slept as
Korigan labored over his studies, and she
dreamed of shared flight. Old Spartish often
advised her to trust in her friend and bide her
time. Patience did not come easily to the half-
wild falcon, especially on days like this, when
the autumn winds were crisp and compelling.
But she could fly, even if Korigan could not,
and grief could not long compete with the
glory of the sky.

Far below the wheeling hawk, Percival,
clinging to the padded cushion of his pillion
saddle, rode along in a much less happy state

of mind. This whole adventure was turning out rather badly, from his point of view. If he, Percival, were to achieve the respect due him as a wizard's familiar, he needed a wizard worthy of his talents. Korigan was definitely not that wizard, and this journey was doing nothing to improve the boy's wizardly skills. He should be home in Sanderstone, studying his spells, not out here in the wilderness playing with a hawk and chasing after unicorns!

And that hawk! That was another thing, fumed Percival. Korigan's falcon was receiving far too much attention and praise for the cat's liking. Hunting was all fine and good— even a wizard's familiar did not disdain the sport. In fact, if the humans would only stop long enough, Percival wouldn't mind doing some hunting of his own. The woodlands were filled with voles: small, snub-nosed rodents that looked very much like mice, but were much tastier and easier to catch.

This pleasant thought lulled Percival back into his usual complacency. With a wide yawn, he settled down for another nap. As Korigan's horse jogged along, the tabby dreamed happily of a midnight prowl, shallow ponds of slow-moving fish, and an after-hunt snack of cream and kippers.

As for Korigan, he couldn't remember a day he'd enjoyed more. Rimko's cheerful manner and ready friendship put Korigan at ease. The young hunter had grown up feeling like an outsider in his own village, yet in one short day, he'd found a place among the Travelers. Already he felt like a valued member of the group. He was glad that Starhawk had hunted so well, for he had a brace of partridges and several plump rabbits to contribute to the evening meal.

The Travelers' queen called a halt promptly at sunset, and the little band set about making camp. Korigan swung down from Bronwyn's back and whistled Starhawk down. As soon as the falcon landed on his arm, a dark-eyed girl edged near. A large brown dog of uncertain parentage followed close at her heels.

Rather shyly, Korigan returned the girl's smile. He'd noticed her during the day, riding bareback on a rawboned mare and guiding the horse without the aid of a bridle. Korigan rode well, but this black-eyed girl seemed to hold wordless communication with her mount.

"Evening, Tasha," Rimko said cheerfully. He handed the reins of his horse to the girl. "I suppose you're off to watch Johann groom the horses, as usual. Do you mind taking ours over to him?" he asked, indicating that Korigan should give her Bronwyn's reins also.

The girl absently took the reins. Her eyes were wide and fixed on the falcon, and her face was alight with wonder. "You trained her to hunt for you. How is such a thing done?" she asked Korigan eagerly.

"What is that to you?" Rimko snapped.

Korigan jumped, startled by his friend's sharp words. He sent an inquiring look at Rimko.

"Our women do not hunt," the boy said casually, as if that explained everything.

Tasha's eyes dropped and the light faded from her face. With a sad smile, she reached out a hand to stroke Percival. To Korigan's astonishment, the cat permitted the caress. Most of the Traveler children and at least half the women had tried to make friends with the grumpy tabby. Percival had met every overture with a hiss of warning. Now, however, he craned his head to the side, purring delightedly as Tasha's slender brown fingers scratched behind his ears.

"You have a gift with animals," Korigan observed gently, hoping to ease her embarrassment.

The girl darted a surprised glance at Korigan. "I suppose so," she said, as if that thought hadn't occurred to her before. She gave Percival's glossy head a final stroke and headed off to the edge of camp, the two horses following obediently behind her.

"Why don't Traveler women hunt?" Korigan asked, as soon as Tasha was out of earshot.

Rimko shrugged away the question. "They never have," he said. "It is not our way." And with that, Tasha was forgotten. The Traveler smiled and clapped Korigan on the shoulder. "Come, my friend. Let's give Starhawk's bounty to tonight's cooks, and then practice with the knives while the light is still with us."

Korigan swallowed his questions and followed Rimko. Just outside the camp they found a dead tree that made an admirable target. Throwing knives required Korigan's full concentration, and he soon put thoughts of Tasha from his mind.

The evening meal was a festive time, with

music and dancing to follow. The girls danced first, their bright skirts swirling around their bare brown feet. When the young men began to dance, arms linked and feet flying, Rimko pulled his new friend into the circle. Korigan felt awkward and embarrassed, for in Sanderstone dancing was not a skill highly valued. The magic of the autumn night soon stole his shyness, and before long he was dancing and laughing with as much abandon as any boy Traveler-born.

Through all this Brucel sat in the shadows, conversing politely with an elderly Traveler but looking sadly out of place. The headmaster made no effort to join the evening's revels. His dignified reserve surrounded him like armor, protecting him from such frivolity. Seeing this, Korigan felt a flash of annoyance at his uncle. This sort of arrogance was so typical of someone from Sanderstone. The people there were so wrapped up in their narrow world of rules and spells, they had little interest in the rest of the world, and even less understanding.

Korigan's feelings must have shown on his face, for when at last he flung himself down to rest, Percival edged close and whispered,

"Things could be worse. The wizard could pull out that duck-call of his and join in with the musicians!"

The mention of Brucel's shawm brought a wry grin to Korigan's face. Rimko sank down beside Korigan and handed him a tin mug of water. "What are you smiling at?" he asked.

Since Korigan had no desire to speak of a tone-deaf wizard and a talking cat, he swept one hand in a wide arc that included the dancing Travelers, the forest beyond, and even the stars overhead.

Rimko nodded in complete understanding. "Life is good here," he said simply, and Korigan found himself agreeing.

When the campfires burned low, a few men melted into the shadows to keep watch. As the Travelers prepared for sleep, Korigan noted that the women tended the fires and the little ones, and the men guarded the camp and repaired the wagons. Labor was divided strictly between men and women, each having a certain role in the life of the camp.

For some reason, Korigan found this deeply disturbing. Even in Sanderstone, with its preoccupation with magic, each person did whatever tasks he or she could best perform.

Elaine Cunningham

Korigan remembered the look on Tasha's face when Rimko reprimanded her, and his unease deepened when he realized why her expression had seemed so familiar to him. She'd looked exactly like he felt, every day that he'd spent in the School of Magic.

He wondered how his friend Aileen would fare in this community of wanderers. Would she be allowed to build her clever inventions, or would the opportunity to develop her talents be denied her? Tasha might have been an excellent falconer, yet because she was a female she could not hunt. This seemed very wrong to Korigan, and the more he thought about it, the more it disturbed him.

Sleep did not come easily to Korigan that night, for too much had happened in the last few days. As he tried to take it all in and sort it through, the effort stretched his weary mind taut as a bowstring. And now, adding to the list of bewildering emotions was a growing sense of disappointment.

Discovering the Travelers had filled Korigan with such excitement and hope. His skills had never been valued, but today they had earned him respect and friendship. All his life he had longed for such acceptance, but now he felt that it might not be enough.

When the next morning dawned—far too soon—Brucel informed Korigan that they must leave the Travelers and go on alone. Korigan was not too sorry to part ways.

Brucel turned their course east toward the mountains. They found a narrow path that wound steeply upward. Before long the path became rough and littered with loose stones, and the horses picked their way carefully. The lush soil of the forest thinned as they climbed, and here and there between the thick pines Korigan glimpsed the rocky bones of the hills. At the base of one sheer stone wall, he noted a small, dark opening. In the forest he was familiar with, there were no caves, and this discovery filled him with excitement.

"Look at that!" he blurted, pointing.

Brucel glanced over. "A cave," he said calmly. "You'll see many more before night falls. These hills are honeycombed with them."

This news sent a prickle of foreboding up Korigan's spine. He raised a hand to rub the back of his neck. "Sounds like prime goblin territory," he ventured.

His uncle shrugged. "You'd think so, but there was no sign of goblins in this area when last I passed through. Nor has word of a goblin settlement reached Sanderstone."

Korigan was not so willing to dismiss the possibility. He carefully marked the location of each cave they passed and watched for the signs and tracks that would confirm his suspicions.

When they made camp that night, Korigan took a small, lumpy sack from his saddlebag and slung a large coil of rope over his shoulder. He whistled Starhawk to his shoulder and strode out into the forest. As an afterthought, he summoned Percival as well.

Setting a brisk pace, Korigan led the way toward the nearest cave. The opening was low, and too narrow for him to squeeze through. If he were a real wizard, Korigan thought, he could cloak Percival in a spell of invisibility and send the cat into the cave to investigate. If he were a real wizard, he could hear the cat's thoughts and see through the cat's eyes. But since he wasn't a real wizard, he'd have to do the best he could.

Korigan was in the process of carefully removing the contents of his bag when Percival finally puffed and wheezed his way up the small hill. The cat cast a wary look toward the cave. "If you think I'm happy about this . . ." he began.

"Trust me, it could be worse," Korigan said wryly. He held up one of the small objects and studied it with a mixture of admiration and loathing. It was a miniature trap, crafted in perfect detail down to its tiny, cruel teeth. Aileen had made fully two dozen for him. Korigan hated traps and refused to hunt with them, yet he saw their value in protecting the perimeter of a camp. He could never have carried so many traps if they'd been full sized, and for once his wizardly training provided a solution to a real problem.

He took a tiny scroll from his magic bag and began to read the words of a spell of enlargement, chanting softly until each trap was big enough to ensnare a night-prowling goblin.

That done, Korigan took a small vial from his bag. He unstoppered it and took a sniff. The vial was marked "HUMAN" but as far as he could tell the liquid within had no odor at all.

Percival wrinkled his nose. "What *is* that ghastly stuff? It smells like you, only more so."

"That's good to know," Korigan said fervently. Among her other talents, Aileen was adept at making long-lasting scents, but the resulting odors did not always resemble what they were meant to. Once, Aileen had taken revenge on a boy who'd boldly pinched her by anointing him with "Essence of Fertilizer." The boy had gone around for fully a month smelling like boiled cabbage. Unpleasant, but not quite what she'd had in mind. Aileen had assured Korigan that this particular scent was true-to-name, but Korigan was happy to have the cat's confirmation. He poured some of the liquid into his hand and began to rub a bit of it on each trap.

"Dare I ask?" Percival said dryly.

"The scent of a human will warn animals away from the traps," Korigan explained. He set one of the traps, sprinkled a few dried leaves over it to conceal it from view, and then rose to his feet. "Take note of where I put each trap, Percival, and be sure that you don't step in one of them."

"Hmmph! Not likely, when they stink like a month-dead mouse. Why are you setting traps with one hand and scaring off game with the other? What could you possibly hope to catch?"

"Goblins," Korigan muttered as he set the

trip wire on a particularly nasty trap. "According to the book of monsters in Sanderstone's library, goblins don't have a very good sense of smell."

"Really. Then if there are any goblins hereabouts, let's hope they've read the same book," grumbled Percival.

Ignoring the cat's complaints, Korigan quickly laid the traps in a wide semicircle around the cave's entrance. When two circles of traps had been set and concealed, he moved deeper into the trees and began cutting lengths of rope. He shimmied up the trunk of a pine and tied the end of one piece of rope to the top branches of a nearby poplar sapling.

"What now?" Percival wondered.

"Snares." The boy dropped to the ground and began pulling at the rope with all his strength. Slowly, the supple branches bent to the ground. Korigan secured the end and quickly fashioned the rest of the trap.

Percival's stomach rumbled, loudly. He glanced at the falcon, who had perched on a nearby branch. The sun had set, and night was quickly closing in. Since the falcon was worthless in the dark, thought Percival, Korigan should hunt for the evening meal now and fool with his traps after tending to important matters.

"Is this going to take much longer?" the cat asked plaintively. "Someone really ought to hunt up some supper."

Neither Starhawk nor Korigan took the hint. "Go ahead," Korigan mumbled, intent on his work.

Since Percival was very hungry indeed, he was tempted to do just that. On second thought, he decided he'd better stick around until the troublesome boy had finished setting snares. Percival had no desire to spend the night dangling by his tail from a sapling.

Finally Korigan seemed satisfied. He strode back toward the camp, the hawk perched on his shoulder. Left to his own devices, Percival set off in search of a likely thicket. Fat, lazy brown voles were plentiful in tall grasses and low bushes, and the cat was not inclined to work too hard for his supper.

Percival took his time, hunting and eating in the leisurely fashion he preferred. He took care to avoid the traps, and by the time the moon rose he'd memorized the location of each one.

He was just finishing his supper when he

heard a scrambling, thumping sound coming from the direction of the cave. Several voices began to converse in high-pitched, scratchy whispers. The sound was like human speech, but even more unpleasant.

For several long moments, the cat weighed his natural curiosity against his equally compelling desire for self-preservation. Finally, with utmost caution, he crept toward the cave, ears back and body so low that his plump belly swept the ground. What he saw made him long to be back in safe, comfortable Sanderstone.

A dozen or so goblins huddled together in the clearing just outside the cave. Their bright red eyes flickered like nervous flames as they peered into the deep forest shadows.

Percival had never seen goblins before, but he'd heard enough about them to recognize the creatures. They looked a bit like humans, albeit much smaller and, on the whole, considerably less appealing. In the faint moonlight, most of them appeared to be the color of mustard, and their skin had the bumpy texture of a toad's. Large pointed ears framed heads too large for their sinewy bodies, and their faces were flat, with broad noses and wide mouths full of sharply pointed teeth. Without exception, the creatures were dressed in smelly leather armor and armed with rusty weapons that had no doubt been stolen from previous victims.

The cat could easily guess the fate of those victims. Goblins were not known for their dainty appetites, and unwary travelers were always welcome at their tables. Or, more precisely, *on* their tables. For all Percival knew, the creatures even ate higher forms of life. Such as cats. And Percival had no intention of ending up in a goblin stewpot.

On the other hand, he could hardly let the goblins attack the camp without making some effort to stop them.

Silently the cat cursed the fate that had assigned him to a head-deaf wizard. If Korigan had any wizardly talent to speak of, Percival could warn him with a silent, mental message. As things stood, he'd just have to think of something on his own. Percival took a deep breath and slunk closer to the hideous creatures.

"Humans!" one of the goblins squeaked, its broad nose wriggling furiously as it sniffed the air. "*Smell* them, I do."

Well, so much for Korigan's monster book, the cat thought grimly as he backed deeper into the forest. Weak sense of smell, indeed!

"Many humans?" inquired another, smaller goblin. Its voice broke on an apprehensive quaver.

"Hope so! Hungry I am," replied the first, striding toward the middle of the clearing. This goblin was taller than the others and walked with a leader's bold swagger.

"You always hungry," grumbled a third, who was distinguished by the dull orange color of its skin. The orange goblin fingered a rusty dagger and fixed an angry glare upon the tall goblin. "Always hungry, always hurry. Always stupid!"

The leader whirled and swatted at its challenger. The orange goblin was ready, and its dagger slashed across the tall goblin's hand.

The creature let out a muffled squeal and hopped up and down, shaking its bleeding fingers. Percival wrinkled his nose in disgust as black goblin blood dripped onto the ground. If possible, the creatures smelled even worse on the inside!

Yet as the cat watched the murderous quarrel, a plan began to form in his mind. He crouched down and waited for the right moment.

With a snarl of rage, the wounded goblin grabbed the orange one by the ears and yanked its face close. Flinging its mouth impossibly wide, the leader lunged forward and sank needle-sharp teeth into its challenger's bulbous nose.

It was the orange goblin's turn to wail, and it did so with energy and conviction. But the leader clung, teeth grinding as it shook its challenger like a terrier puppy tormenting a slipper. Finally the tall goblin flung the defeated creature away and spat into the bushes. The orange goblin scuttled toward the cave, clutching what remained of its nose.

Breathing heavily, the winner glared at the circle of goblins. "I lead," it growled in as deep a voice as it could muster. A dozen bald heads bobbed as the goblins nodded nervous agreement. Satisfied, the leader turned to the forest once more.

"You lead," Percival agreed, speaking in a high, menacing voice. "You lead . . . *for now!*"

The tall goblin's face twisted with rage, and it whirled to face the others. "Who say that?"

Immediately the creatures began to gibber

and point accusing fingers at their neighbors.
After a few moments of this, the leader threw
up its hands and ordered silence.

"Enough! We find humans now. Walk quiet,
circle around. When I say, rush in." The goblin
shook a spiked club and grinned horribly.
"Lotsa stew tomorrow!"

Slowly, cautiously, the goblin band crept
deeper into the forest. They held their weapons before them, ready to fight. Behind them
stalked Percival, who was trying desperately
to pretend that he was still hunting harmless
little voles.

The cat waited until the group was almost
upon the first circle of traps. Then, summon-
ing all his courage, Percival sprang. He nipped
the leader's backside and then darted back
into the trees.

The goblin let out a howl and spun, one
hand clutching at its behind and the other
swinging its club in a wide arc. All those
within reach of the weapon squealed and
dove for safety. Percival heard the cruel *snap*
as two of the goblins fell headfirst into the
waiting traps.

"That my brother!" shrieked a thin, one-
eared goblin, pointing toward one of its dead

comrades. In a frenzy of rage, One-ear dove at the leader. The two goblins went down together, kicking and clawing. All the others gathered around to enjoy the battle. They grinned with cruel delight and made wagers about the outcome.

As Percival watched the fight, it suddenly occurred to him that the thrashing goblins were rolling closer and closer to his hiding place. Soon he would be crushed under the fighters—if he did not first die from the smell! Yet how could he run, with the eyes of a dozen well-armed monsters turned in his direction? One way or another, he was in grave danger.

This is it, the cat thought grimly. I'm stew.

But then a shrill cry split the night, and a dark form hurtled down from the sky like a winged nightmare. The goblins scattered, shrieking in alarm. Even the two combatants paused, fists upraised and expressions of terror frozen on their ugly faces.

"Starhawk?" muttered Percival, who was as surprised as the goblins by the arrival of the fierce bird. Later, the cat vowed, he'd have to find out how and when the falcon had taken up night flying. At the moment, however, Percival had an opportunity and intended to use it.

With a yowl, the cat leaped upon the two remaining goblins, raking and scratching and biting. This was too much for the frightened creatures. They jumped to their feet and dashed into the trees. Percival followed closely, nipping at their heels like a border collie herding some particularly troublesome sheep.

A satisfying snap ended the career of the goblin leader. To Percival's surprise, old One-ear was proving the greater challenge. The crazed goblin simply would not be herded. It darted here and there like a caged squirrel.

Again Starhawk flew in low, slashing with beak and talons at the frantic goblin. Percival immediately closed in on the other side. Between the two of them, they managed to nudge the one-eared creature toward one of Korigan's snares. With a crisp *whoosh*, the sapling snapped back to its normal posture. The goblin swung by one ankle, windmilling its arms and gibbering curses.

The cat and hawk took no time to admire the results of their teamwork. Together they hunted down the goblins and chased them, one by one, into the waiting snares. By the time the first rays of morning touched the eastern mountains, a fine crop of goblins dangled from the trees around the cave.

With deep satisfaction Percival surveyed the night's work. Most of the goblins had fallen into snares and would free themselves in time, but the cat planned to be long gone before then. He took one final nip at a suspended goblin and then padded wearily toward the camp.

It was a long walk for the tired cat, and the forest looked very different in the morning light. He might not have found the humans at all, had not Starhawk wheeled and circled over the camp like a beacon of welcome.

Korigan looked up as the cat stumbled into camp, and his eyes widened. Percival's fur—usually so glossy and meticulously groomed—was matted with brambles and sticky with foul-smelling black goo.

"What happened to him?" Brucel demanded, eyeing the bedraggled cat.

It was on the tip of Korigan's tongue to say he didn't know. But then, that would be admitting he couldn't talk mind-to-mind with his familiar.

To his relief, Starhawk spared him from answering. The falcon swept into the camp with a plump wood duck in her talons. The falcon dropped her prey, not at Korigan's feet, but next to Percival! Starhawk then settled down on a nearby rock and waited.

The boy's eyes narrowed as he studied the hawk and the cat. The two creatures regarded each other steadily, if from a wary distance. Then, with a shrill cry, the falcon lifted off into the sky. For no reason that Korigan could understand, he had the distinct impression that a truce had been drawn.

He looked up at Starhawk, and as he gazed at the soaring falcon his mind flooded with strange and alien sensations: the wild pleasure of the chase, the comfort of a newfound companion. Korigan glanced down at Percival, who had curled up by the fire and promptly gone to sleep. Suddenly, the boy's mind filled with borrowed memories that pictured the bedraggled tabby as a fierce, stalking hunter.

As suddenly as it had come, the vision was gone. Korigan took a deep breath. He accepted what he had received, even if he did not fully understand it. With a smile, he turned to his uncle and said, "While we slept, Percival has been out hunting!"

* * * * *

A little while later, when Brucel was busy tending and saddling the horses, Percival awoke. The cat yawned hugely and began his after-nap stretch. "You needn't bother about your traps and snares. Those that I didn't fill with goblins, I sprung," he muttered sleepily.

Korigan's jaw dropped. "Goblins? You filled the traps with goblins?"

"What else? Of course, goblins! And do you think I'm happy about it?" the cat complained, now fully awake. "I've nipped more goblin ankles and backsides than I can count. It would take a cowful of cream to get that horrible taste out of my mouth! At the very least," he amended, glancing pointedly at the morning campfire, "some nice roast duck?"

A wide grin split Korigan's face. For the first time, he admitted that Percival might become the familiar that he'd always wanted. The cat showed unexpected courage and resourcefulness. He might even have saved all their lives!

"After what you did last night, you can have anything you want!" Korigan promised.

"I'll keep that in mind," the cat said dryly.

"For the moment, however, I require only three things: some breakfast, a bath, and at least ten miles between me and goblin territory."

5
The Staff of Thorn

As Korigan and his companions descended the mountain, the rocky outcropping and ridges gave way to a deep pine forest. The morning passed quietly enough, and when the sun was high in the sky the sound of rushing water beckoned them. Ahead was a mountain stream, with a waterfall tumbling into a clean, clear pool. A pair of raccoons harvested crayfish along the shore.

Eagerly the thirsty horses pressed through the brush toward the water. The crackle of dry leaves and the gurgle of the mountain stream filled Korigan's ears, and his eyes were fixed on the water ahead.

Perhaps that was why they didn't see or hear the wolf until they were almost upon it. The creature bared its teeth in a snarl and crouched low, ready to spring.

Brucel's mare reacted first. The gray horse screamed with terror and reared so sharply that the wizard tumbled from the saddle into a thicket. Korigan grabbed his bow and leaped from Bronwyn's back before he, too, could be thrown. As his frightened horse cantered back toward the path, Korigan fitted an arrow and sighted down the wolf. The young hunter's eyes narrowed as he studied the animal, and slowly he lowered his bow.

Meanwhile, Brucel had risen to his feet and snatched up his fallen magical staff. The wizard's face creased with deadly concentration as he leveled the staff at the wolf.

"No!" shouted Korigan.

Even as the protest burst from his lips, Korigan dropped to one knee and fired. His arrow hit Brucel's staff and sent it flying from the wizard's hands. A flash of green light sizzled harmlessly toward the clouds.

The wolf snarled and snapped. Brucel drew

the dagger from his belt and braced himself for the attack. When the attack did not come, he cast an angry but curious glance toward his nephew.

"Whatever were you thinking about?" demanded the wizard.

The boy did not answer, for his attention was fully absorbed by the wolf. The animal had neither attacked nor fled, *because she could not*.

A crude leather harness bound the wolf's shoulders, and the reins had become hopelessly entangled in the bushes. How long she had been caught, Korigan could only guess. The wolf was terribly thin, and patches of her fur had been worn off by her struggle to free herself.

Goblins, Korigan thought grimly. They were known to use worgs—an evil and much larger cousin of the wolf—as willing mounts and allies. This she-wolf was too small and too wild for such treatment. She had escaped the goblins, only to find a new captivity. Anger coursed through Korigan at the thought of what the animal had endured.

Slowly, carefully, Korigan edged forward. The wolf cringed, and bared her teeth in a weak snarl. The boy thought of Spartish, and he remembered how the old man had handled frightened animals. He began to speak to the wolf in a low, soothing murmur, gazing directly into her golden eyes.

The wolf whimpered as Korigan drew near, and trembled when he touched her, but she did not bite or even growl. The boy took a pot of herbal salve from his bag and gently smoothed some on her wounds. Then, talking all the while, he took his hunting knife from his belt and cut the leather harness. The wolf gave his hand a quick, grateful lick and then limped off into the forest.

The boy rose and turned to face his uncle. "She'll be fine now, as long as—" He stopped abruptly, startled by the strange light in Brucel's eyes.

"We might not have to do this thing," the wizard muttered excitedly. "There might be a better way!"

Brucel snatched up his staff and gestured to his nephew. "Come, Korigan. Find the horses and let us be on our way at once. We must change course and go deep into the forest."

"What is it, Uncle?"

"If what I suspect is true, then a unicorn might yet be allowed to live!"

That was all Brucel would say, and for a time Korigan was too busy hunting down the horses to ask questions. Once they were mounted and on their way, he was hard pressed to keep pace with the wizard.

Brucel led the way into the forest, finding a section of woodland that was deep and impossibly thick. Soon they had to walk and lead the horses, for there was no path that Korigan could see. After a time, he noted the ancient oaks that stood at regular intervals along the way, like silent sentinels. Gnarled and ageless, the trees seem to watch them as they passed.

By late afternoon, they came to a glade filled with golden light, for the sun filtered down through countless layers of autumn leaves. Mist clung to the grass and rose from a low, stone well in a gold-tinted cloud. Brucel went immediately to the well and dipped up a bucketful of water. He drank deeply, reverently, and then began to refill their flasks. Korigan, however, stared in wonder at the cottage on the glade's far side.

Built from stone and covered with climbing

vines, the little dwelling looked as if it had grown from the soil. The cottage was nearly identical to the house that Korigan had grown up in. All it lacked were his mother's neat beds of herbs. Instinctively, Korigan took a deep breath. A familiar, spicy fragrance filled his senses.

Wonderingly, he followed the scent to the back of the cottage. There, overgrown and untended, were more herbs than Korigan had ever seen in one place. Most were familiar, some he recognized only from his mother's descriptions. Of these he gathered seeds and samples, carefully placing them in the tiny linen bags he always carried into the forest. Korigan could picture his mother's delight as she added these plants to her gardens. The thought of her made him anxious to move on, though the peace and beauty of the glade urged him to linger.

"Korigan, come within!" called his uncle from inside the cottage, and Korigan reluctantly followed the call.

The house was orderly and sparsely furnished. Dust lay thick on the few pieces of furniture, and cobwebs roped the rafters, but for some reason Korigan did not need such signs to know that no one had lived in the cottage for some time.

Brucel went to a corner and took up a staff of light-colored wood. It was simple, with none of the ornate carvings and mystic runes that decorated the wizard's staff. Yet Brucel handled the smooth wood with reverence.

"This was your father's staff," the wizard said, and he handed it to Korigan. "It is now yours."

For a moment Korigan felt as if he'd been plunged into an icy lake. He knew nothing of his father, apart from the whispered speculations of the villagers. As he took the staff, Korigan's head whirled with a thousand unanswered questions. He managed to give words to the most important one.

"Who was my father?"

"His name was Thorn, and he was chief druid of this land."

Brucel paused, as if lost in memories. "Your mother is not a wizard," he said at length. "She has another, rarer gift. As a girl, she was much like you, taking every opportunity to roam the forests. One such time, she met Thorn. He recognized in her the druid's gift and accepted her as a student. In time, they grew to love each other and were married."

"My father was a druid. And my mother, as well," Korigan said in a dazed murmur. So that was why the forest called to him so! That was why he'd always felt so out of place in the wizardly confines of Sanderstone. If only he'd known, how much misery he would have been spared!

"Why did Mother never tell me this?" the boy demanded.

"She could not. Thorn died before you were born, and it was his wish that you not be told of your heritage. A druid's path is often lonely and hard, and he would not have you take it upon yourself unless you found your own way to it."

Korigan nodded slowly. In Sanderstone, it was assumed that a child would follow in the footsteps of either one or the other of his parents. If he had known that both parents were druids, Korigan would surely have sought this path from his earliest years, and his father's last wish would have been denied.

"Then why do you tell me now?"

"When your mother returned to Sanderstone, she understood that you would be given a wizard's training. She even hoped, as

I did, that you might take to the life. Although you have learned a bit of magic, it is clear that your heart is not in it," the wizard said. "Over the years, I've often thought you might have the druid's gift. After watching you tend that wild wolf, I have little doubt. I pray that it is so, for a true druid need not kill the unicorn to claim its magic."

Korigan sank down onto a dusty chair. "I don't understand."

"If you are Thorn's son in spirit as well as in blood, then you need only ask for the gift of healing. To those who dwell in harmony with the forest, the unicorn gives freely of its magic. Remember the legends, boy! The touch of a unicorn's horn confers magical blessings—even water so touched becomes life-giving magic! But in these days, unicorns fear mankind, and rightly so. The few unicorns who yet live have retreated to sacred glades, and nowadays only druids learn the secrets that unlock these havens.

"But enough of such talk," the wizard said, his voice almost gay. "The unicorn hunt awaits!"

* * * * *

Intent on the path ahead, the hunters rode swiftly away from the druid's glade. Had they lingered and looked deep into the well, they would have seen a ripple pass through the still, dark waters. It was a gentle movement, but powerful enough to send a message.

And because all waters are one, and all things are magical to those who see, the message was received.

Not far away, in a valley deep-shadowed by looming mountains, the surface of a pond trembled as the magic moved through it. After a time the pond stilled, and the silent waters waited for a response to the message it had passed along.

Without a sound, without a ripple, a unicorn rose from the pond and waded to the shore. The unicorn shook her wet head, scattering droplets like shards of crystal that caught the sunlight and tossed it about in tiny rainbows.

Like all of her kind, the unicorn was vain, and she leaned over the pond to enjoy her own reflection. As her mane dried, it tumbled down her long, slender neck in silvery ringlets. Her milky-pearl horn was whorled like a shell, and pointed like a stiletto. She shook each cloven hoof, and admired the silky white hair that feathered about each foot. Although often described as a white, horned horse, the unicorn resembled a horse only as an elf resembles a human. Like her elven counterpart, the unicorn was infinitely more delicate and graceful, with a slender strength and a fey nature. Magic lingered about her like an aura, enhancing her beauty and her wisdom.

At length the unicorn looked past her reflection, seeking out the message that had been sent to her. She had not had word from the druid's glade in many years, and she studied the water carefully. The unicorn's heart leaped with joy as the meaning of the summons became clear to her.

So the Great Druid's staff had been taken. And by his son! The unicorn rejoiced in the thought that another druid might soon claim the glade. She had known many druids over the centuries, but none had been as cherished as Thorn. If this boy was Thorn's son in spirit as well as in blood, the unicorn might soon have another companion.

Despite her delight, the unicorn was cautious. Although her kind longed to love the humans and bring joy and magic to their short, bright lives, the unicorns had too often been betrayed by those they wished to aid.

And so the unicorn would follow the boy, and she would watch. And finally, she would judge. The price would be her life if she bestowed her trust in error, yet this was a price the unicorn was willing to pay.

The unicorn had been too long alone.

6

A Druid's Cat and a Dragon's Tracks

"A druid! Just when I thought things couldn't possibly get any worse, I find myself saddled with a druid," Percival grumbled for what seemed like the hundredth time.

"Would you please be quiet!" hissed Korigan over his shoulder. It was late afternoon now, and the cat had sulked and complained steadily since they left Thorn's glade. "Look up ahead there; Brucel is starting to give you odd looks."

"And why shouldn't he? I'm a laughing-stock," the cat returned bitterly. "A druid has no more use for a familiar than a *dog* has for a *brain*! Once news of this gets around Sander-stone, I might as well give up and set myself up in some mouse-infested barn as a farm cat. I'm finished as a familiar, I tell you. Finished!"

Where complaints were concerned, how-ever, Percival was far from finished. The cat kept up a steady stream of them as the shad-ows lengthened and the forest grew thinner. Gritting his teeth, Korigan fixed his eyes on the path ahead and did his best to ignore the tabby. The boy thought about the staff that he'd secured to the saddle in a makeshift baldric of rope and cloth, and he wondered what powers the druid's staff might hold. And most of all, he wondered whether he, Korigan, could learn to wield those powers.

But despite his wandering thoughts, Kori-gan kept a close watch on the trail with eyes made sharp by years of hunting and tracking. As the blue of the autumn sky began to fade to silver, Korigan noted that the ground under Bronwyn's hooves was beginning to soften. Overhead, waterfowl flew in stately V-shaped formations, their honking calls bidding a plaintive farewell to their summer lands.

And then, stretched out before Korigan, was the moor. Like a vast lake of golden grasses and purple heather, it lay between two ranges of rugged mountains. In the fading light, the far mountains were wreathed with autumn mist in sunset shades of purple and rose.

It was more beautiful than Korigan had imagined possible. And the hunting! Starhawk would be in her glory here! The boy shook the reins over Bronwyn's neck to urge her forward.

Brucel flung out a restraining hand. "Do not ride onto the open moor," he said sternly. "It looks solid, but amid the grasses and flowers are bogs that can swallow a man whole. There is a path where we can cross safely, about a league to the north."

"But there is path right over there," Korigan said, pointing to a strip of flattened grass. "Someone has passed through, and not long ago. And they built a campfire—see the blackened grasses over there?"

The wizard's eyes were not so keen as his nephew's, but he squinted in the direction

Korigan indicated. A look of deep concern crossed his face. He swung down from his horse and strode over the path. After a moment he beckoned Korigan over.

"You have never seen these tracks, but you will know what they are."

Korigan's eyes widened. The soft, marshy ground held a series of large, three-toed prints. Each footprint was deep, indicating a creature of great size. Korigan stared in awe at the evidence of a beast that, until this moment, he had only half believed existed.

"A dragon?" he breathed.

Brucel nodded grimly. "And you won't tame it as you did the she-wolf. Such a creature is outside the persuasions of a druid." The wizard pursed his lips and gazed out toward the blackened circle. "How odd. The dragon was on foot, and it seems as if it were pursuing something—"

"A stag," Korigan supplied, pointing to the smaller, sharp prints that marked a frantic zigzag toward the blasted grass.

"And the dragon killed its prey with its fiery breath," the wizard mused. "Stranger still. Dragons are intelligent creatures, far too intelligent to risk using fire in grasslands. It's a marvel the moor didn't go up in flame."

Korigan reigned Bronwyn closer to the tracks. He leaned in for a better look at the trail. The heel of each print was deep and sharp, suggesting that the dragon had moved slowly. The dragon's back claws had scored deep furrows, as if it had dragged its feet. Korigan pointed this out to his uncle.

Brucel nodded thoughtfully. "That explains much. According to legend, a great red dragon has been laired somewhere in these caves for hundreds of years. It must have awakened recently, and its lack of judgment in the use of fire indicates that it was desperate with hunger."

"And weak," Korigan added, pointing to the sluggish tracks.

"Strong enough," the wizard said grimly. "Although I would doubt that the dragon can yet fly, it is a fearsome foe. On the open moor, we are vulnerable. We must be away from this place at once."

Brucel mounted his horse and then removed a silver ring from his finger. "This holds a spell that will transport us across the moor, to a path on yon mountain. Stay close, and take care to keep the hawk with you."

The wizard spoke a few arcane words and then tossed the ring into the air. It disappeared with an explosion of white light. Korigan clapped his hands to his eyes too late to keep the sudden bright light from stealing his vision. He had no sensation of movement at all, and Bronwyn's strong back was solid and still beneath him. Yet when his sight returned, Korigan looked out upon a very different scene. His horse now stood on a rocky mountain path, high above the moor. Korigan grinned, delighted with the adventure even if it *was* the result of a wizard's magic.

His companions were not so pleased. Shrieking, Starhawk burst into flight, and Bronwyn pranced and whinnied. For several moments Korigan struggled to keep his seat and to get his horse under control. All the while, Percival clung to his back like a giant burr.

"Ouch! Let go," Korigan demanded, but Percival only dug his claws in a bit deeper and hung on.

As soon as Bronwyn was calmed, Korigan reached over his shoulder and peeled off the cat's paws, along with a good bit of his own skin. Angry, he held the cat before him at arm's length. Percival was still obviously shaken by the abrupt journey. His ears lay flat back against his head, and every hair stood on end, making the cat look twice his normal size. His yellow tail was fatter and fluffier than Korigan would have imagined possible. Percival hissed at the boy, but his heart clearly wasn't in it.

Korigan felt a certain sympathy for the frightened cat. He lowered Percival to his lap. As he stoked the cat's fur, a thought occurred to him. He turned to his uncle and asked, "If you could do that, why didn't you just transport us right to the unicorn's glade?"

"The glade is not like most places," Brucel replied. "It cannot be breached by a wizard's magic, and it is difficult for the finest woodsman to find. Perhaps Thorn's staff can help us find a way in."

"Wonderful," muttered Percival from Korigan's lap. "It's bad enough that we're ten leagues north of nowhere. Now we're following a stick."

The wizard shot a puzzled look at the cat, and then reined his gray mare toward the summit of the mountain.

"Keep your voice down, for the love of mice!"

Korigan hissed angrily, once Brucel had ridden out of hearing range.

Percival seemed impressed by the boy's choice of words. Nevertheless, it was the cat's nature to disagree. "Nonsense. I barely purred."

"Then I think Brucel can hear you. You know—like I'm supposed to?"

"Mind-to-mind? Impossible," Percival stated, his tail lashing decisively. "If every wizard had access to a familiar's thoughts, how would wizards keep secrets from each other? Imagine the chaos if every passing apprentice could pluck spells from the mind of a powerful wizard's familiar! And what of the familiars, I ask you? Would-be wizards would be forever capturing us and expecting us to spill trade secrets. We cats would not stand for it, I assure you. We value our privacy too highly. We are familiar to one wizard, and that," Percival concluded bitterly, "is often more than enough." The cat cast a sour look at Brucel. Apparently Percival intended to hold a grudge over the teleportation incident.

"Then you're talking too loud," Korigan insisted.

The cat had just begun to argue that point when, with a rush of wind and a fierce beating of wings, Starhawk dove toward them. Percival meowed in startled protest as he abandoned his place on Korigan's lap and scrambled back onto the pillion. Korigan barely had time to slip on his leather glove before the falcon dropped onto his wrist.

"What is it, Starhawk?" Korigan whispered, for she was more distressed than he'd ever seen her. Her talons clutched frantically at Korigan's arm, yet her wings rustled as if she were restless for flight.

Korigan flung his arm up, tossing the falcon into the air. She traced a tight circle overhead, as if uncertain whether to fly or settle. Finally she disappeared over the mountain ridge. Feeling extremely uneasy, the boy pulled off the glove and tucked it back into his belt.

"Come look at this," Brucel called from the path ahead.

The trail rose up the mountain, steep and narrow. Korigan urged Bronwyn up to the wizard, and noted that their path joined a second, much larger trail. On it Korigan saw the marks of the Travelers' wagons.

Korigan was about to point this out to Brucel when he was seized by an overwhelming desire to flee. He clutched at his temples and struggled to beat back the panic. Never had Korigan known such terror. His vision swam and spun, and suddenly the moor below was no longer a sea of gold and purple, but a sharply detailed, black-and-white landscape. Somehow Korigan understood that the image was not his own, nor was the fear.

Moving as if in a daze, Korigan once again pulled his falconer's glove from his belt and thrust his hand into it. He held out his arm, bracing it with his right hand, just as Starhawk plummeted from the sky. The falcon's wings beat furiously to slow her descent, yet still she hit Korigan with a force that almost knocked him from his horse.

Brucel looked at the boy with narrowed eyes and an unreadable expression. "What did the falcon see?"

"The dragon."

The words came out without thought, but immediately Korigan recognized them as truth. "The dragon has eaten well, and has gained the strength to fly," he said with growing certainty.

Korigan pointed to the wide path. "The Travelers passed this way. They may be in danger." He stiffened as claws dug once again into his back; Percival had chosen this moment to climb to Korigan's shoulder.

"I can almost guarantee that," the cat muttered in Korigan's ear. "Look up there, over the canyon."

Filled with foreboding, the boy did so.

Flying in tight circles over the mountain pass, silhouetted against the sunset sky, was the dragon.

7
Spell Battle

However long he might live, whatever adventures he might yet face, Korigan knew he would never forget his first glimpse of the dragon.

Yes, he'd seen them pictured in the *Monstrous Encyclopedia* in the library of Sanderstone's wizard school, but no painted illustration could have prepared him for the fearsome beast that wheeled and circled over the canyon.

Overlapping red scales—every possible shade of red, from ruby to rust—covered the beast's body and neck. Plates of gleaming, red-bronze armor ran across its belly. Iridescent wings shaped like those of an enormous, crimson bat beat the air with a noise that rivaled thunder. With each stroke, the glittering wings caught the last rays of sun and tossed them out in streaks of multicolored light, like beams from a dancing prism, or sparks from a flame. The dragon's head was crowned with curving black horns, and the paws curled under its massive body sported talons like daggers.

Just when Korigan thought he could not possibly be more awed, the dragon roared. The sound started with an ominous rumble, rolled into a shriek, and finally exploded into a burst of smoke and flame. And Korigan, who had never known a moment's fear of any living creature, knew Starhawk's terror as his own.

But Brucel leaped from his horse and ran up toward the crest of the mountain. "Follow me!" he shouted at Korigan. "We must act quickly, or the Travelers will die!"

That broke the spell of fear that bound the boy. But Bronwyn shrank against the side of the mountain, and Korigan could do nothing to ease her terror or persuade her to leave the safety of the rocky ledge above her. Nor could he move, for his leg was pinned firmly between the horse and the wall of rock.

Percival came to his rescue once again. The cat leaned over the back edge of the pillion saddle and raked his claws across Bronwyn's rump. With a startled snort, the mare shied away from the wall. Korigan promptly slid off her back.

"Stay with Bronwyn," he commanded Starhawk and Percival.

"That goes without saying," the cat muttered.

Korigan began to follow Brucel up the steep path. On impulse, he darted back and grabbed his father's staff. He scrambled over the rocks to a narrow ledge near the summit of the mountain. Far below them, in a narrow box canyon, was a ring of brightly painted wagons. The Travelers were without cover . . . and without hope.

For the dragon had folded its wings and begun to dive.

A burst of green light flashed toward the dragon. Korigan whirled, to see Brucel standing behind two large rocks. His wizard's staff was pointed at the dragon and still smoking from the blast.

Brucel's magical fire nearly missed the beast, but it struck the tip of the dragon's tail. A searing hiss filled the air. Again the dragon roared, this time a shrill cry of rage and pain that seemed to vibrate through Korigan's very bones.

The dragon pulled out of the attacking dive and climbed higher in the sky, lashing its scorched tail as it went. It circled once, then flew straight toward the wizard.

"Get behind the rocks!" Brucel shouted, and his hands began to flash through a series of complicated gestures.

Korigan dove for the scant shelter, rolling behind the rocks just as the wizard finished his spell.

And suddenly, all sound stopped: the thumping *whoosh* of the dragon's wings, the sweep of wind that followed the creature, even its horrible roar. So complete was the silence around them that the rapid beat of Korigan's heart thudded loudly in his ears. Wonderingly, the boy rose to his feet—and clunked his head against an invisible barrier.

At that moment fire poured from the sky. Korigan instinctively dropped to the ground and flung his arms over his head. To his surprise, the killing blast did not come.

After a moment, Korigan ventured a peek upward. He and Brucel were surrounded by a bowl-shaped dome of livid flame. The wizard's spell had created a magical shield that turned away the dragon's fiery breath.

They were safe for the moment, but their little shelter was becoming painfully hot. Sweat poured down Korigan's back, and his uncle's face glowed a deep red above his black beard. And still the fire came on and on, and the heat grew more intense as the dragon flew ever nearer. The surface of the magical shield began to bubble like melting glass.

"The shield can't last much longer!" Korigan cried.

"It doesn't have to." The wizard took a small vial from his bag and muttered a few arcane words. He then reached out and snatched an arrow from Korigan's quiver. With quick, precise movements, he twisted off the arrowhead and replaced it with the ensorcelled vial.

"When the dragon pauses to take another breath, shoot this directly into its mouth," the wizard said grimly. "You've got only one chance, so make it count."

Korigan instinctively hefted the arrow to test its balance. The new arrowhead was a crystal vial, filled with a glittering purple liquid, yet the young hunter felt sure that the arrow would fly true. "But the shield—"

"Is thinning," Brucel said, finishing the boy's protest. "It will not survive another such blast. The arrow should be able to penetrate it."

Should? Korigan did not want to think about what might happen if the arrow could not. He fitted the missile to the bowstring, raised his bow, and waited.

Finally the firestorm ceased. The dragon's flight had taken it past their magical shelter, and the beast was climbing higher into the sky and circling around for another pass. Korigan hoped that the dragon would turn fully around before letting loose its next blast. He had to have a clear shot before the second attack began, for the dragon's fiery breath would reduce the arrow to ash before it even came close to its target.

Suddenly the dragon turned. It wheeled sharply, and its massive head reared back in preparation for the attack. The bronze-plated chest expanded as the dragon drew in air to fuel the next firestorm.

Korigan pulled back the arrow. He took a deep breath, held it, and released. The magic arrow shattered the wizard's shield and flew straight toward the dragon's open mouth.

With the shield gone, the sounds of the dragon's attack bombarded Korigan like thunderbolts. The pounding thump of wings, the crackle of the flames simmering in the dragon's throat, even the sharp *pop* as the magic vial exploded in the dragon's mouth— all were so loud that Korigan could *feel* the sound.

Most powerful of all, however, was the rushing, sweeping sound of the gathering winds. For when the magic arrow exploded, it stole the energy meant to fuel the dragon's attack. Air rushed in to fill the void, racing into the dragon's mouth with the force of a whirlwind. It flung the creature backward, so powerfully that the dragon's wings clapped together in front of its belly, folding like prayerful hands. Immediately the dragon began to plummet toward the canyon floor.

The startled dragon let out a thunderous belch, and its wings flapped wildly as it struggled to regain control of its flight. It recovered and once again climbed into the sky. The dragon's huge wings beat more slowly now, with a ragged rhythm, and it flew directly away from the dangerous humans.

"He's had enough," Korigan said with deep relief. "He's leaving."

But at that moment, the dragon began to hiccough. Its enormous red shoulders heaved as it sent puffs of smoke into the sky. An ominous rumble began in the dragon's throat as this latest indignity renewed its rage. With a fierce scream, the dragon spun around and flapped back toward Brucel and Korigan.

The dragon could not breathe fire, nor could it fly close enough to the narrow ledge to dispatch its prey with tooth or talon. After several circles overheard and several roars of frustration, the dragon came to rest on a broad stone ledge not too far below. The gaze it fixed upon the two humans was terrible and compelling.

Korigan clutched the rocks and stared down at the angry creature. Fear gripped him like a huge fist, squeezing his breath and stealing the strength from his limbs.

"Wizard!" the dragon roared between hiccoughs. "Do not for a moment think that you have won. Know that fire is but the least of my weapons—and tremble!"

Korigan did not have to be told twice. He was already shaking like an aspen tree in a summer storm. He was only dimly aware of Brucel's hand on his shoulder, of his uncle's deep bass voice shouting into his ear.

"Whatever you do," the wizard demanded, "don't look into the dragon's eyes! Dragonfear can overwhelm you—strong men have died from sheer terror."

But the boy could not tear his gaze away. The malevolent golden orbs drew him, pulled him to a place beyond fear or reason. Korigan was certain that he would die. He *deserved* to die, for next to such majesty and power, he was nothing. Weak with terror, he fell to his knees. Still he could not look away. Moments passed—or perhaps hours—as Korigan drowned in the despair of dragonfear.

Slowly a voice came to him, as if from a great distance, as if through water. From the corner of his eye, Korigan saw Brucel holding out to him a thin, flat rock.

"Break the slate!" the wizard shouted. "Use Thorn's staff."

Korigan summoned all his strength and tried to free himself from the dragon. Try as he might, he could not pull his gaze from the dragon's eyes. But he clasped the staff and raised it high, struggling for every inch he gained. With a final great effort, he slammed the druid's staff onto the flat slate. The rock split down the middle, and suddenly Korigan was free. Exhausted, he slumped to the ground. The staff slipped from his hand and tumbled unheeded down the steep path.

A tremendous rumble split the air as the ledge under the dragon cracked and gave way. Rocks tumbled and rolled down the mountain. Deprived of its perch, the dragon labored into the sky. Korigan, who had spent hours studying the flight of birds, knew at once that the dragon was in trouble.

"The dragon is hurt, or perhaps just not yet strong enough to fly well," he told Brucel. "If you could hit it with one more magical missile, you might be able to knock it from the sky."

The wizard nodded. "Thorn's staff. Get it for me at once!"

For just a moment, shock froze the boy. Hadn't Brucel said that only a druid could wield the staff? Korigan wasn't sure what the wizard intended to do with it; nonetheless, he scrambled down the incline after the fallen staff.

He snatched it up and hurled it like a javelin toward the wizard. Brucel deftly snatched the staff out of the air and pointed it, not at the dragon, but toward a fluffy sunset cloud.

Korigan watched, scarcely breathing, as the cloud clenched in upon itself like a fist. The tight-packed cloud brooded, turned gray, and then spat bolt after bolt of lightning.

The wizard's aim was true, and lightning streaked a jagged course toward the dragon. A horrible, lingering scream filled the sky. The dragon spiraled down toward the canyon floor; one of the crimson wings was blackened and useless, and its tattered shreds flapped like ribbons as the creature made its final descent. When the dragon hit the canyon floor, the impact shook the mountain and threw Korigan and Brucel to the ground.

Korigan found his feet first, and offered a hand to help his uncle rise. The two looked down into the canyon. Far below them, the dragon lay motionless.

Korigan saw some of the Travelers race up to examine the fallen creature. Their songs of triumph soared upward through the still evening air, and Korigan let out a huge sigh of relief.

"We did it," the boy murmured. "I don't know how, but we did it!"

"The druid's staff is a powerful force," the wizard replied softly. Brucel's eyes lingered on the staff for a long moment before he handed it back to the boy, and something in the wizard's face persuaded Korigan to hold back his questions. They walked in silence down the path to reclaim their horses. When they were mounted and on their way down the mountain, Korigan could no longer restrain his curiosity.

"I thought you said that only a druid could wield Thorn's staff," he ventured. "Yet you knew what to do."

His uncle rode in silence for several minutes. "Do you consider yourself a wizard?" Brucel demanded.

Korigan blinked, startled by the unexpected—and seemingly pointless—question. "Not really. No. Of course not," he concluded firmly.

"Yet you can work some magic, and cast some few spells. How is that so?"

"How else?" Korigan responded, puzzled by this line of questioning. "I've studied at the School of Magic for more than five years! I might not be much of a student, but I've learned a few things!"

"Just so," the wizard agreed. After a moment's silence, he added, "Your mother did not go alone to the Great Druid's glade. In my youth, I thought that I might also have the druid's gift, and I trained with Thorn long enough to gain a little of the lore and the magic. Since there are among druids those who excel in bardic arts, I even attempted to learn something of music. You have heard me play the shawm, so you know how well those studies progressed," the wizard said, with a touch of wry humor.

"But my path lay beyond the druid's glade," Brucel concluded briskly. "As does ours."

There was little Korigan could add to that. They rode in silence until the light faded, and then they made camp on a rocky ledge, much like the one that the druid's staff had shattered.

Long into the night Korigan lay awake, counting stars and savoring the discovery of his heritage and his identity. He was the son of Thorn, the Great Druid, and now his father's staff—and all its powers—belonged to him. The boy's fingers stroked the worn wood of the staff, and his mind raced with plans for the future.

Yet when sleep came at last, Korigan's dreams were filled with the roars of a hunting dragon.

8
Mountain Folk

Korigan and his companions were on their way before dawn. They were making good time along the ridge that connected two tall mountains when Bronwyn, who was in the lead, simply stopped.

The roan mare froze, and a tremor ran through her strong back. The reins were pulled from Korigan's hand as the horse lowered her head in a deep, reverent bow.

Korigan was not much of a wizard, but he had been around powerful magic all his life, and he felt its presence now. Slowly, wonderingly, he raised his eyes to the mountain ahead.

There on the very summit, silhouetted against the sunrise, was a unicorn. Korigan's breath caught in his throat. Once again he could not look away from a magical creature, but this time wonder, not fear, held his gaze.

The unicorn was more beautiful than Korigan had imagined possible. Her coat gleamed like pearl in the first rays of sun, and her long graceful horn reflected back the pink of the sunrise clouds like a shimmering mirror. She reared, pawing the air with gestures more graceful than a dancer's, as if she were celebrating the morning and her own beauty.

And then, the unicorn turned her deep, wise eyes fully on Korigan. Time stopped as unicorn and boy gazed at each other, and measured, and tried to understand. What knowledge of him the unicorn gained, Korigan could not say, but for him the moments he spent linked with the unicorn brought a flood of joy and insight beyond anything that he had ever known.

For the first time in his life, Korigan understood a wizard's love for magic, for the unicorn was the embodiment of all things magical. Yet the unicorn possessed a wildness, a natural power that was totally foreign to the strict rules and memorized spells of Sanderstone. This magic, Korigan knew, was the magic of the forest, the waters, and the sky. The magic of the unicorn was the magic of life itself.

Korigan heard Brucel's whispered expression of awe, and he understood why the powerful wizard had once desired to pursue the druid's path. Korigan marveled only that all men did not seek out the unicorn's glade. For the first time in his life, Korigan felt his father's presence beside him, for surely this link with the unicorn was the greatest joy of a druid's life. In it Korigan read the confirmation of his new dreams and plans, and a promise of healing for his druid mother.

As if sensing his thoughts, the unicorn tossed her silvery mane in what seemed to be a nod of affirmation. Once more she reared, and then she turned and disappeared over the crest of the mountain.

Korigan felt no sense of loss, for he knew in his heart that he would meet the unicorn again. They would find the unicorn's glade, and there they would gain the gift of healing for Korigan's mother. And ever after, his life would be defined by this moment. Nothing, Korigan vowed, could disturb the sense of magic and peace that filled him now.

And then a spear thunked solidly into the trunk of a pine tree, not more than an arm's length before their eyes.

The weapon was still quivering when a mountain woman stepped onto the path before them. The woman was short and dark, with browned skin and fierce eyes. She was about the same age as Korigan's mother, and nearly as small—seemingly far too small to have thrown the wicked spear. Yet she was armed for battle, with a short sword strapped to her hip and a hand axe at her belt. Her leather armor was well fitted and well-worn. The woman stood with her fists on her hips, eyeing the travelers.

"You're not *dwarves*," she said, fairly spitting out the word, "and you're not of these mountains. You've no part in this war, so what brings you into the midst of it?"

"We are merely riding through," Brucel assured her. The wizard's eyes were still fixed on the spot where the unicorn had been, and his voice out came in a hushed, distracted whisper. "Our village is isolated, and we had not heard that there was trouble with the small folk."

"Trouble? Trouble enough!" the woman snapped. "The greedy little diggers opened the old mines near Rommelwither's lair. After seven hundred years of peace, the dragon has been awakened. The dwarves will pay in blood for that!"

"Then rest easy, for the debt has been paid," the wizard replied. "And in a currency far more appropriate than dwarven blood! The dragon is dead. Its body lies in the canyon just below this ridge."

The woman nodded slowly. "So that's what all that commotion was about. We saw strange lights and sounds over yon mountain, but thought it might be the dwarven forges, preparing weapons for the battle ahead."

"Of the dwarves and their plans, we know nothing," Brucel murmured.

"But the dragon is dead, you say? By whose hand?"

"We killed it," Korigan blurted out. "My uncle and I did, that is."

The fighter's eyes widened, and she turned to Brucel, her hands clasped before her. "Such a thing could be done only by powerful magic. Then you are a wizard, my lord?" she asked eagerly.

The wizard finally dragged his gaze away from the unicorn's ridge. His shoulders lifted and fell in a deep sigh.

"I am," he said. His voice was stronger now, but held a note of resignation. Korigan heard it and understood.

"Can you tend my daughter?" the woman implored. "She was wounded in battle with the dwarves. The cut has turned angry, and naught I do can ease her. My lord, will you see to her?" Her voice was no longer that of a tough warrior, but a mother beseeching help for her child.

Regret flooded Brucel's face, and for the first time his attention fixed fully upon the mountain woman. "Alas, I have little knowledge of the healing arts."

But Korigan thought of the herbs in his bag, and the salves and potions his mother insisted that he carry with him always. Although he had never seen a battle wound, he thought there might be something he could do.

"If your home is not far, I will see what

might be done," Korigan offered.

The woman's eyes flashed over Korigan, and her shoulders slumped. "Not far," she said dully. It was plain that she had little hope in the youth's skill, yet she was not about to turn away any help, any chance her daughter might have.

She was true to her word. The small cabin lay just over the ridge. Its sole occupant was a girl about Korigan's age, as brown and wiry as her mother. The girl lay on a pallet before the fireplace, and her sleep was far from easy. Her head tossed restlessly and her thin face burned with the flush of fever.

Korigan quickly went to work. He had the woman boil some water and steep healing herbs. Then he showed her how to bathe the wound with the soothing potion. While the woman tended the girl, Korigan pounded certain plants into a paste and mixed them with porridge meal and dried herbs to make a poultice that would help draw off the poison. He gave the mother a tea, made from the bark of a certain tree, that would ease the fever and the pain. Finally, he sent Starhawk off hunting for rabbits. A thin, rich broth made from the meat and some special herbs would help to restore the girl's strength. Korigan had often seen his mother cook pots of this healing broth for ailing villagers, and he knew the making of it as well as did his mother.

Hope dawned on the woman's face as she listened to Korigan's clear, confident instructions. The young man's work already showed results, for the girl seemed to be resting easier.

"It's grateful I am, young lord," the woman said, and her grim face softened as she gazed at her sleeping daughter. "All I have to offer you in return is a warning. Don't continue along the ridge to yon mountain, but take the trail that goes down into the canyon and up the other side. The fighting with the dwarves is far from over, and the ridge is an important passage." She nodded toward her wounded daughter. "You see before you part of the price of defending it."

"But why continue to fight, when the problem has been resolved? The dragon is dead," Korigan reminded her.

The woman shrugged as if this were of little consequence. Korigan noted the expression on her face and did not try to pursue his logic. In Sanderstone, he had grown accustomed to the villagers' unshakable confidence in their ways of doing things. The mountain woman wore that same look of righteous superiority, and he knew better than to try to reason against it.

Apparently Brucel also recognized that brand of stubbornness, for with scant ceremony he ushered Korigan out of the cabin and onto the path that led down the mountain.

"The detour will add half a day to our travels," the wizard said grimly as they rode as fast as they dared along the steep, rocky trail.

"Then why not continue on the ridge?" asked Korigan.

"If we do, we might not reach our destination at all," Brucel said. "The woman spoke truth when she said there would be trouble. Under that ridge lies a warren of dwarven mines, and the fighting there could become fierce. Mountain folk and dwarves don't get along at the best of times. Now that they actually have an excuse for a war—not a good one, mind you, but a poor excuse is better than none—it's hardly safe to ride over a dwarven stronghold."

And since there was nothing else to be

done, the companions picked their way down the mountain and into the canyon where the dragon had fallen.

9

Old Friends and New Paths

Joyful cries greeted them long before they reached the Travelers' camp. A crowd gathered around Korigan and Brucel, singing a song praising the "mighty dragon slayers." In turn, each Traveler pressed into their hands a bit of jewelry or a coin. Most of the girls kissed Korigan on the cheek as they offered their thanks. The boy's face grew redder with each kiss, and he longed to dive into one of his saddlebags.

Although Korigan was embarrassed by the

reception and the gifts, he read in Brucel's stern gaze the message that he must accept both. Even so, a future druid had little use for gold and gems, so when the song was finished, Korigan slipped the treasures into his spell component bag, where they could keep company with all the other things that he would no longer need.

The Travelers were in a festive mood and had no desire to move from the canyon. Yet, when Brucel and Korigan insisted that they could not stay for the celebration, the Travelers decided to ride along and bring the celebration with them. The camp was packed in short order, and in minutes the caravan began to make its way up the steep mountain road.

Several of the Travelers played gay tunes as they rode up the treacherous mountain path. Fortunately, they were expert riders, guiding their horses with their knees so that their hands were free to play their fiddles, rebecs, and mandolins. Korigan thought this a most useful technique and tried it with Bronwyn. After a few puzzled moments and frustrated snorts, the horse got the idea and began following the new instructions.

Korigan had just begun to relax when familiar claws dug a path up his back. He grimaced and braced himself for Percival's latest complaint.

"Nice party, wouldn't you say?" the boy murmured with polite sarcasm.

"Do you think I'm happy about this?" Percival complained in Korigan's ear. "After all I've been through these last few days, the least you could do is try to grant me a little peace and quiet so I could take a nap!"

"You have had a nap already this morning," Korigan pointed out. "In fact, you've had two or three of them, and it isn't even highsun yet! For once, why don't you quit complaining and just try to enjoy things?"

The silence behind him was too long and too heavy. Korigan had begun to regret his suggestion when the cat said sweetly, "Why Korigan, what a wonderful idea. By all means, let's add some amusement to this little shindig."

At that inauspicious moment, one of the Traveler's lively ballads wound up with a wild strumming of the mandolins and the high, lingering wail of a fiddle. Percival cleared his throat and spoke into the silence.

"Uncle Brucel, why don't you play next?"

the cat said, raising his deep voice to imitate Korigan's uncertain tenor.

The boy's face turned as red as a summer apple. He made a grab for Percival, but the cat had leaped back down to his pillion seat. Timidly, Korigan cast a glance in his uncle's direction. When he caught sight of Brucel's expression, the boy began to understand what Percival was about. Never had Korigan seen the powerful wizard so nonplussed.

Brucel's jaw was slack with astonishment, and his face was as bright a red as Korigan's. When the wizard cast a glare of venomous inquiry in Korigan's direction, it was all the boy could do to hold back an amused smirk.

The Travelers began to clamor for a song. Brucel tried to withdraw gracefully, but the Travelers would not be put off. Finally the wizard relented and pulled his shawm from its bag.

The Travelers fell silent as the plaintive voice of the shawm wandered its way around the edges of a tune. Their dark eyes were serious and they listened with respectful faces, but Korigan noted that they took care to avoid each other's eyes. He well understood, for if anyone looked at him right now, Korigan knew that he would burst out laughing. Behind him, Percival purred in short bursts of feline mirth.

Then slowly, tentatively, the voice of a fiddle joined the shawm as one of the Travelers began to pick out the wizard's ragged melody. A guitar joined in, providing harmony with softly strummed chords. Soon several tambourines kept time, and a dozen gypsy girls hummed a haunting, mournful harmony. One by one, the Travelers joined in, transforming the dreadful performance into a thing of beauty. Surrounded and supported by the gypsy music, the mistreated shawm sounded better than it ever had before, or was likely to again.

When the song ended, the entire caravan of Travelers burst into applause that was both gracious and genuine. Brucel inclined his head in a slight bow and then quickly tucked the shawm out of sight.

The Travelers turned to storytelling, apparently thinking it the safer entertainment. One by one, they told stories full of whimsy or adventure.

Korigan listened intently as each Traveler shared a story. When it was his turn to speak,

Korigan saw no reason not to reveal the purpose of his journey. After all, he was traveling to the unicorn's glade on a druid's pilgrimage to ask for the blessing of healing, not as a hunter to kill the sacred and magical creature.

And so Korigan told them all that had happened on the trip, from the encounter with the brigands to the battle with the dragon. He told them of the war brewing between dwarves and mountain folk. He told them of his mother's illness, and the village healer's belief that only a unicorn's magic could heal her. Finally, he told them that he had actually seen the unicorn. His announcement was met with awed silence, and then respectful applause.

With Korigan's tale, the storytelling session ended and the Travelers began to talk softly among themselves. The queen, bareback on a spotted mare, rode to Korigan's side.

"We were all greatly impressed by your story. In these days, few men would think to ask a boon of a unicorn," the queen said, and her dark eyes searched Korigan's face. "Why do you think the unicorn will grant you this gift?"

In response, Korigan pulled the druid's staff from its place behind his saddle and held it out before him.

The queen's eyes widened in surprise. "That is the staff of the Great Druid!"

It was Korigan's turn to be surprised. "You knew him?" he asked eagerly.

"Many times the Travelers have been guests in the druid's glade. He was a fine man," the queen said.

The praise warmed Korigan's heart. "He was my father," he said with quiet pride.

"Ah." The queen sat silent, studying Korigan. "So you are Thorn's son. That explains much, but not all. And what will you do, son of Thorn, once you have found the unicorn and taken the gift of healing to your mother?"

"I'll seek out a druid to be my teacher, and once I have learned what I must know, I will return to Thorn's glade," Korigan replied, confident in his newfound path.

"I see." The woman's dark eyebrows rose skeptically. "And there you will remain, in one place, for the rest of your days?"

"Yes," he said decisively. But the queen's questioning scrutiny continued, and Korigan shifted uncomfortably under her gaze.

Finally the woman looked away. "We Travelers will part company with you at the top of this mountain," she said casually. "Your quest will lead you toward the north, and we are bound eastward, to the Iceflow River."

Korigan's heart quickened. For years he had read stories of the legendary Iceflow River, and he had indulged in many a daydream about testing himself against its dangers and challenges. The river was long, and it wound its way through exotic kingdoms and untouched wilderness. It traveled through wild mountains, and its white-water stretches had claimed the lives and the treasures of many an adventurer. Fearsome monsters made their lairs in the caves along its shore, raising the odds against those who would try to recover such treasure. Just the mention of this river rekindled Korigan's lifelong dreams of adventure and travel.

"Tell me about the river!" he begged. "Have you ridden the white water? What lands have you traveled through? What monsters have you met along the way? Do you think the stories of treasure are real, or merely tavern tales?"

The queen threw back her head and laughed

delightedly. Before she could respond to the flood of questions, however, Rimko reigned his black stallion next to Bronwyn.

"Come, my friend," he invited Korigan. "We can practice with the daggers while we ride. Throwing while riding is a good skill to have."

Maybe, Korigan admitted silently, but such a skill was of little use to a future druid. "Thank you, but no," he said politely.

Rimko looked surprised, but he merely shrugged and rode off alone toward the front of the caravan.

"You should have gone with him," said the queen. "Better to hone your skills than spend too much time listening to an old woman's tales."

The memory of his eagerness to hear just these tales made Korigan feel a little guilty. What need did a future druid have for the Iceflow River, or for wild adventure in distant lands?

"Throwing knives is not a skill that I will need," Korigan said firmly.

"Who can say?" the woman replied with a smile. "You hunt well with the bow and the hawk, but it never hurts to learn new ways."

"I have no need of a hunter's skills. I am

159

going to be a druid, like my father," Korigan said stiffly.

"Perhaps this is so, but where is it written that you can do nothing that does not fit the role you have chosen? And why must you become one thing only?" the queen demanded. "You are not that now. You are a hunter and a master of hawks. You know more of herb lore than many a Traveler healer or midwife. You follow a trail as well as any man I've known, and you ride as if you were born in the saddle. You even know a little about the magic of wizards."

"*Very* little," Korigan muttered.

"Sometimes a little magic is enough."

Korigan agreed with a nod and a grim smile. "As to that, I agree. A little magic is more than enough."

The queen chuckled. "I can see that a wizard's life is not for you. You must return to your Sanderstone, but once your mother is healed you should not stay. A tomb or a town, it is much the same to you."

"I don't intend to stay in Sanderstone," Korigan said impatiently. "I told you, I plan to become a druid."

"But you are young, and you may yet choose

otherwise. What road can you choose, that you have not traveled? Taste them all!" the queen advised. "Perhaps you will find a single path that you love above all others; perhaps you will always love best the road that lies yet before you."

Korigan thought about her words, and his desire to see the Iceflow River returned in full force, burning in him like a fever.

"And what destination does the Queen of Travelers hold in her heart?" he asked.

"You know the answer to that," the woman said, and laid her brown hand on his shoulder. "You know it as well as any Traveler born. The joy is in the journey itself."

Korigan did not know how to answer the queen. Part of him agreed with her words, and part of him clung to his newly minted dreams. After a moment the queen patted his shoulder.

"Go now, and practice throwing daggers with my Rimko. In my long life, I have learned that knowledge is never wasted."

Korigan nodded politely and did as he was bid, but he was not entirely convinced that the queen's words were true. He saw little value, for example, in his years of training in

Sanderstone's School of Magic. And what had Brucel's druid training earned him, beyond a longing for a gift he could not possess?

That question haunted Korigan as the caravan made its way up the mountain. When it came time for him and Brucel to part ways with the Travelers, Korigan accepted Rimko's gift of four throwing daggers and exchanged vague but sincere promises to meet his friend again, "on the road."

When he was finally alone with his uncle, Korigan turned to Brucel and spoke his mind. "All that time you spent training with Thorn. Do you ever regret it?"

"Not at all," Brucel replied. "Although I do not possess command of a druid's magic, even a limited knowledge has served us well. No knowledge is wasted," he said, unconsciously echoing the words of the Traveler's queen. "It is extremely odd for a future druid to possess the weapons and instincts of a hunter, yet if it were not for your skill with the bow, we would have been destroyed by the dragon's fire."

The wizard smiled wryly. "Who knows? You may even find a use for your magical studies," he added, as if he had read Korigan's mind.

Korigan doubted it, but felt it would hardly be wise to say so.

His questions answered for now, he lapsed into silence. To help pass the time, he took the chunk of flint from his bag and began to chip and flake it into a proper arrowhead. Finally he held it up and examined it with satisfaction. The surface of the arrowhead was still a bit rough, but it would do the trick.

Brucel reached out to take the stone from him. "Isn't this the spell component you need for throwing fire?" he asked sharply.

Korigan shrugged. "So?"

"You should have learned that lesson. Throwing fire is a valuable spell to know."

"Maybe," the boy agreed as he reclaimed his arrowhead. "But if I'm to be a druid, I'll have no use for such things."

"But you *will* need arrows?" Brucel demanded sharply.

That question floored Korigan. Indeed, what use did a druid have for a bow and arrow? How could he live in harmony with the forest's animals, if he was a hunter?

The boy opened his mouth to respond, but he found that he had nothing to say. So he merely shrugged again, and was grateful when the wizard did not pursue this disturbing line of thought.

As the sun climbed high in the sky, Korigan's stomach began to rumble. He sent Starhawk up to hunt for the midday meal. The falcon took to the air with a shriek of delight.

And suddenly Korigan, too, was airborne. Although Bronwyn's back was still strong and solid beneath him, the boy's senses expanded to include a dim perception of Starhawk's feelings and sensations. He felt the crisp rush of autumn wind, the freedom of the sky, and the joy of flight.

Korigan closed his eyes and rejoiced in his union with the wild hawk. Surely this meant that his druidic powers were emerging, perhaps awakened by Thorn's staff.

Despite his delight in his shared flight and in his growing power, the boy found himself frustrated, and wished that he had learned about his heritage long before this trip. How much more he would know now, if he had begun early to walk the druid's path. How much frustration he would have been spared: five long years in the School of Magic studying spells he could not master, all the while feeling as out of place in Sanderstone as a hen in a duck pond. So much time wasted.

And yet, Korigan mused, Brucel had done much the same thing, and the wizard did not consider the detour a waste of time. Despite the years his uncle had spent studying in the forest, he had still attained Sanderstone's highest rank. Perhaps in time he, Korigan, might even take his father's place as Great Druid.

The boy's pleasant dreams were interrupted by a stronger, more vivid image. Through eyes that were not his own, Korigan saw rushing waters, and a deep pool with shadow-hiding trout. He took a deep breath, and the vision was dispelled.

"There's a stream not far over the ridge," Korigan told Brucel. "Let's stop there to water the horses. Starhawk would like some fish, and I'm sure Percival wouldn't object to such a lunch, either!"

The wizard's head snapped around, and he fixed a startled gaze on his nephew. "You see this up ahead," he stated softly.

Korigan shrugged. "Starhawk sees it, I guess, and somehow passes it along. It's hard to describe."

"Oh, I think I understand," Brucel said

dryly. "Tell me, how long have you been able to do this?"

"Not long. Just an odd impression or two, the past few days. It's getting stronger, though. Is this because I have Thorn's staff, do you think?"

Brucel did not answer. He did not seem to have heard at all, for he rode in silence, wrapped deeply in his own thoughts.

Korigan did not mind the wizard's reverie, for he had much to think about, himself. But as he lost himself in dreams of the future, questions emerged that only Brucel could answer. Korigan was eager to claim his heritage and develop his power, yet since his father was dead, at whose hand would he receive his training?

"After Thorn, who became the Great Druid?" Korigan asked. "Where should I go to begin learning what I must know, in order to take my father's place?"

The wizard did not look up. "Keep your mind on the purpose of our quest," he said brusquely. "There is time enough to consider your path, once the unicorn hunt is completed."

10
Familiars

As they made their way down the mountain, the terrain became rougher, and the trees grew thick and dark overhead. Korigan felt that he should be comforted by the familiarity of a forest, but for some reason he was not. There was danger here, of that he was certain. What that danger might be, and how he knew of it, he could not say. Without giving the matter much thought, Korigan took his bow from his shoulder and placed it across his lap.

A snarl was the only warning Korigan got,

but it was enough. He snatched up his bow and fired into the trees.

There was a moment's silence. Then the body of a mountain lion fell to the path ahead. Shot through the heart, the animal had died at once. Its mouth was still flung open in a snarl, and lethal claws extended from the limp paws. The lion was a male, full grown and larger than any Korigan had ever seen.

"Now *that's* what I call a cat!" Percival muttered from behind Korigan's back.

Brucel turned a puzzled stare in the boy's direction. Suddenly, Korigan realized what he had done, and how it must appear to the wizard. He cast the bow away as if the weapon burned his fingers.

"I shot without thinking," he said defensively.

"Your instincts served you well," Brucel replied quietly. "The lion would have attacked us. Pick up your bow, and let us ride on."

"I don't want it," Korigan said, shuddering as he looked at the dead lion.

"Whether you want the bow or not is hardly the point," the wizard said sternly. "You will need it more than once before this journey is over. Now pick it up!"

The Unicorn Hunt

Korigan knew better than to argue when the wizard used that tone. He reluctantly retrieved his bow and hung it in its accustomed place over his shoulder. He rode along in grim silence, brooding over what he had done. How could he ever become a druid if he could kill with such skill and ease? He should have sensed the lion's presence, and persuaded it not to attack. Korigan had seen Spartish, the beast master of Sanderstone, talk a wild skunk out of spraying. If a town-dwelling wizard could do as much, why could *he* not do better?

At that moment Starhawk flew heavily to his side. In her talons was a plump grouse. The falcon settled on the ground beside Korigan and waited expectantly for her praise and her portion.

Korigan slid from the saddle and accepted Starhawk's gift. He quickly prepared the grouse and fed the falcon her favorite tidbits. All the while, he waited for the sense of revulsion to return. It did not. Try as he might, Korigan could not fault the falcon for either her choice of food or her love of the hunt. Starhawk was being true to her nature. He could expect nothing else of her.

Brucel watched as Korigan fed and praised the falcon. "Starhawk's devotion to you is commendable," the wizard observed. "She would be a far better familiar than the cat. At the very least, she knows enough to show a bit of respect."

He cast an acid glance toward the napping tabby. Percival opened one eye and returned the wizard's glare, then he wrapped his tail across his face and returned to his nap.

The reference to Percival puzzled Korigan, for the cat had been more discreet with his insults of late. But the boy had more disturbing matters to consider, and he didn't give his uncle's words much thought.

As the afternoon wore on, Korigan's uneasiness increased. He had a premonition that a danger far greater than a hunting lion lay ahead. They rode steadily toward the pass, however, for Brucel insisted that the unicorn's glade lay ahead, in the valley just beyond the next mountain.

But as they neared the pass, Korigan began to understand the source of his concern. He saw the signs left by booted feet, and then, bright even among the colors of the fallen autumn leaves, drops of blood. Korigan slid from Bronwyn's back and followed the gory trail to a clearing that had been trampled flat by dozens of feet—some large, some small—and stained with splotches of darkening crimson.

From a bed of golden ferns Korigan pulled a small, blood-stained axe. A dwarf had fallen here, and though his kin had borne him away, the weapon told the tale of the small warrior's fate. No dwarf that still drew breath would willingly leave his axe behind.

With respect and sadness, Korigan returned the axe to its resting place and made his way back to the path.

"There has been fighting here," he told his uncle. "And not long ago. The dwarves have retreated toward the pass. Is there any other road that we can take?"

Before Brucel could answer, Korigan's sharp ears caught the sound of distant battle. The sound came from behind, on the trail above them. Then, from the forest, came the clashing of swords.

"They are all around us!" Korigan said.

"Send Starhawk up to scout," Brucel suggested. "Perhaps she can show us a safe way through the battle."

"But only once or twice have I actually *seen* what she sees, and then only a glimpse," Korigan protested. "That is not enough to guide us!"

"Remember your lessons," the wizard said sternly. "You have been taught how to enter into rapport with your familiar. Do it with Starhawk, and do it now."

Korigan was doubtful, but he did as he was told. He closed his eyes and sent a silent command to the falcon, putting behind it the force of concentration learned by long, tedious practice in Sanderstone's classrooms. Slowly, the falcon's mind opened to his.

Before this moment, Korigan had received only echoes of Starhawk's feelings, glimpses through her eyes. Now he shared fully in her freedom and her joy of flight. His vision sharpened, too, and through the falcon's eyes he saw the landscape in a detail he had not thought possible. He saw the rabbit grazing far below, and felt the quick, strong surge of hunger and temptation. Korigan sent a message of urgency to the falcon, telling her that they must find a path through the battlefield at once.

In response, the falcon climbed higher into

the sky and began to circle. Through Starhawk's eyes, Korigan saw the horror of his first battle.

On the path ahead, a small band of mountain folk struggled to regain the pass, but one by one they fell to dwarven axes. In the forest to the west, the humans fared somewhat better; though their swordsmen were overmatched, dwarves also died as arrows sang from thickets and trees. On the path behind Korigan, another group of dwarves had banded together with a pair of hill giants. The giants hurled boulders, crashing them into the ranks of the mountain folk below.

Through the falcon's sharp eyes, Korigan could read the hatred and the fear on every face. Then, suddenly, his vision settled upon a face that he knew.

It was the mountain girl, the one whose wound Korigan had treated. A sling and bandage bound her right arm, but she determinedly swung a sword in her left hand as she charged up the hill toward the dwarves. Korigan watched helplessly as the girl went down under a giant's rock.

Sickened and dismayed, Korigan longed to break away from Starhawk and the disturbing vision she shared with him. And frightened though he was, he burned with a desire to rush into battle beside the mountain folk he had aided. Yet if he did, he and Brucel would likely die alongside them, and with their deaths his mother's hope of recovery would also die.

So the boy again urged Starhawk to seek a passage through the battlefield. The falcon climbed into the sky, glided, and sent her answer down to Korigan. Her task completed, she dropped to Korigan's outstretched wrist.

"The battle rages all around us," Korigan said in a dull, empty voice. "We can do nothing to help, nor can we escape. But there is a cave not far from here. Perhaps we can take shelter there until the fighting stops."

Brucel nodded. "Excellent. If I'm not mistaken, there may well be a path for us there."

Korigan led the way, following the path he had seen through Starhawk's eyes. At the mouth of the cave, Brucel raised his wizard's staff and spoke a few arcane words. A halo of green light rose from the end of the staff, turning it into a magical torch. The wizard peered into the cave and nodded in satisfaction.

"It is as I suspected. This must be the entrance to one of the dwarven mines. It may well lead us through this mountain."

"But the dwarves—"

"Are otherwise occupied," Brucel said dryly. "Perhaps they left fighters to guard the mines, but we will deal with that problem when and if it comes."

The two riders dismounted and led their horses into the cave. In the light of Brucel's torch, the rocks glowed an eery green. The cave narrowed into a tunnel, and an acrid stench filled the air. Their boots crunched with each step.

"Bat guano," Brucel said with a mixture of disgust and relief. "This is no dwarven mine. Say what you will about dwarves, they would not allow this mess to accumulate in one of their tunnels."

"So what is this passage?"

"Probably one of the tunnels that leads toward the dragon's lair," the wizard admitted.

Percival stirred restlessly on his pillion seat and cast a murderous glare at the wizard.

Despite the gravity of their situation, Korigan grinned. "For the first time, I wish I could hear your thoughts," the boy muttered to the cat.

"No you don't," Percival responded grimly. "Trust me on this." And the tabby lapsed into a moody—and highly uncharacteristic— silence that lasted several minutes.

"That's enough!" Brucel suddenly snapped. "Korigan, do something about that wretched cat! I've endured his snide remarks for far too long."

"But Percival didn't say anything," Korigan said in a puzzled voice.

"What do you mean, he didn't—" The wizard broke off suddenly. "Oh, of course. Since Percival is not your true familiar, you wouldn't be able to hear his comments. And you can count yourself lucky for that," he concluded in an acid tone.

Korigan was about to explain about the cat's talkative gift when the truth dawned on him. "But you *can* hear Percival, mind-to-mind! That means that Percival is *your* familiar!"

Brucel gaped, then grimaced. "It does, doesn't it?"

He regarded the cat, who looked no more pleased at the idea than did the wizard. "Do you know how long it's been since I've had a familiar?" he muttered.

The cat's eyes narrowed into slits. Brucel looked surprised, then he let out a bark of laughter.

"It's been a long time since someone dared to insult me," the wizard said, but he sounded far from displeased by this observation.

"I have a feeling you won't have to wait so long for the next time," Korigan said dryly.

"How do you know—" The wizard broke off and smiled. "Of course. I'd almost forgotten that cats can talk, if they want to."

"Which we usually don't," Percival put in sourly. "And that's the last you'll hear from me!"

Korigan grinned, delighted to be rid of the last vestige of his wizardly training. "Is that a promise?" he asked Percival.

"Yes," the cat said. "And that *is* my final word. Except for this," he added. "There's a light coming from the passage up ahead to the right. If I were leading this little stroll through futility—which unfortunately I am not—I would investigate."

Korigan squinted down the side passage. Sure enough, there was a faint light at the end of it. They turned into the tunnel, and were relieved to find it free of both bat droppings and dwarven guardians.

The tunnel turned sharply at the end, and suddenly they were in the light of bright midday. When their eyes adjusted, they found that they had emerged from the tunnel into a beautiful, grassy valley.

"Is this the unicorn's glade?" Korigan asked eagerly.

"Not quite," Brucel said in a somber tone. "But we are close."

They mounted their horses and began to ride toward a copse of trees. As they came to a deep pool, Korigan felt again the unmistakable presence of magic. And on the saddle behind him, Thorn's staff began to resonate with power.

11

The Unicorn's Mirror

"What is this place?" Korigan whispered, pointing to the water.

"The pool is sacred to druids," Brucel said. "Many young druids make pilgrimages here."

"Why?"

"Does it matter?" the wizard said impatiently. "We have more important matters to attend. Let us ride on."

"No. Not yet."

Korigan slid down from his horse. He took the druid's staff from its holder and, walking to the water's edge, gazed into the pond. Although the surface was calm and silvery, it seemed that a spring bubbled deep in the water.

"What is this place called?" he asked.

With a sigh of resignation, the wizard dismounted and came to stand at Korigan's side. "This is called the Unicorn's Mirror. It is a sacred pool where the unicorn can communicate with druids, observe sacred sites around the world, even search out other unicorns. This they do seldom, for unicorns live solitary lives. Yet from time to time they seek the company of their own kind."

"If they did not, there would be no baby unicorns," Korigan observed.

"Quite," the wizard agreed dryly.

"But there is more to the pond than that," the boy said, pointing with Thorn's staff toward the underwater spring.

Brucel sighed again. "Somehow I knew you would ask about that. Some say it is a path to the unicorn's glade. That it is a passage of some sort is certain. It is a path a druid must travel, a test he must take before claiming his full powers."

Korigan gazed at the bubbling passage, as

if his sharp eyes could penetrate the secrets of the druid's spring. A look of determination settled upon his face.

He cast aside the druid's staff. Before Brucel could stop him, the boy plunged into the pool.

The shock of icy water momentarily stole Korigan's confidence. Down he sank, numb and motionless. He quickly regained his resolve, and though his limbs felt wooden and stiff, he began to swim hard toward the bubbling spring.

Korigan's lungs burned with the need to breathe. He rolled on his back and glanced up. Far above him the blue of the sky beckoned with the promise of air, and of life. But Korigan turned back to the druid's spring and put all his remaining strength into one final great effort. His legs churned the icy water, and his hands stretched toward the mystic passage.

And then the spring was all around him. Korigan gulped in a mouthful of the bubbles, hoping to find in them a bit of air. To his surprise, it worked. No longer desperate for breath, he became aware of the passage around him. And with this awareness came the knowledge that his ordeal had only just begun.

Korigan tumbled helplessly, caught in a whirl of air and water. Then the bubbles dissolved into something else, a whirling vortex that was neither air nor water. A roar louder than a dragon's filled Korigan's ears, and colors brighter than the wizard's fire spun around him. Korigan flailed, but there was nothing to grab, nothing to slow his descent.

For falling he undoubtedly was. On and on Korigan fell, and the pressure built until he felt his ears would surely explode and his body crumple from the force of the magic that gripped him. Slowly, painfully, even Korigan's sense of time was squeezed away.

Everything he had ever done, every thought and every sensation, pressed in upon Korigan at the same time. He felt the weight of every moment of his fourteen years of life, without past and present to organize them into any meaningful pattern.

Desperately, he began to search for just such a pattern. He would become a druid, like his father before him, like his mother the gentle healer. He would go through this passage, and he would emerge in the unicorn's glade, or he would willingly die.

Yet try as he might, Korigan could not fit his life into the pattern he desired. His daydreams about travel and adventure returned to him, twisted into horrific nightmares. Every arrow he had ever shot reversed course and came back to pierce him. Aileen was there, laughing wildly as she hurled ball after ball of magic fire at him. The Travelers surrounded him, and their brown hands beckoned and clutched at him from all sides. Rimko appeared, his black eyes mocking Korigan as he hurled his knives into him, one by one. With the detailed clarity of the falcon's vision, Korigan saw again the war between the mountain folk and the dwarves. His own battle rage came back to him, burning through his veins like fire. Percival's raking claws tore at his eyes, the cat's derisive purr mocking his torment. But the most terrible pain of all came when Starhawk turned on him.

The falcon grew and grew until she was the size of the dragon that Korigan had helped to slay. As Starhawk descended upon him, Korigan knew the terror that every quail and rabbit had felt when the falcon's shadow fell upon it. Korigan the hunter had become prey. He was fit for no more than this.

In despair, Korigan abandoned his struggles. The wings of the giant falcon surrounded him, and her talons gripped his body. As her open beak dove toward his heart, Korigan surrendered to the darkness.

12

The Hunter

"Do you think I'm happy about this?"

The familiar question came to Korigan as if from a great distance. Slowly, painfully, the boy fought his way back toward the acerbic voice.

Korigan coughed, and water rushed from his mouth and nose. He gasped in huge breaths of air, savoring it even though it burned its way into his lungs.

With a great effort, he opened his eyes. His vision swam and blurred, for he was still partially blinded by the unearthly light of the druid's passage. When at last he could see, he looked up into the concerned faces of his uncle and Percival. Water dripped from the wizard's beard, and the usually fastidious tabby looked comically small and bedraggled with his long yellow fur plastered to his body. Korigan was lying on the soft grasses on the edge of the pool, and overhead was the lifegiving blue of the sky.

Korigan tried to speak, but all he managed was a groan.

"So you survived," Percival said in his usual dour tone.

"I almost wish . . . I hadn't," Korigan gasped out. Every inch of his body ached, and his limbs felt as heavy and lifeless as scrap metal.

Brucel heaved a sigh of relief and raked a hand through his wet hair. "I should have known better than to let you near that pool. How would I ever have faced Maura, had you not lived!" he fretted.

"It's not your fault. I did what I did," Korigan said.

"As did I," Brucel replied with a grim smile. "Do you think you were the first to fail the test of the Unicorn's Mirror?"

Korigan struggled to sit up, but the wizard eased him back. "Since you will not be content until you have heard all, you might as well rest while I tell you the story," Brucel said dryly.

"As you know," he began, "I once studied with Thorn. You also know that I did not have the druid's gift. During my training, I occasionally suspected that this might be true. Yet I was headstrong and proud—much like you—and I also challenged the pool and its secrets."

The wizard fell silent for a long moment. "I did so right after my first trip with Thorn to the unicorn's glade. That trip was to have been a rite of passage, since the gift of a unicorn sighting is often granted to druids. I did not see the unicorn."

"But I have seen the unicorn already!" Korigan protested.

"We both did," Brucel reminded him. "The meaning of that gift is not yet clear to me, but I know beyond questioning that I am no druid. And now," he concluded gently, "you know that you are not, as well."

Korigan shook his head, not ready to accept what he knew to be true. "But I saw the unicorn," he argued. "And when I did, I felt that she knew of my quest and approved!"

"I think it unlikely that a unicorn would underwrite its own demise," Percival observed dryly.

Brucel winced, but did not contradict the cat. Korigan observed this and tucked the fact away for future examination, but he was too numb to explore the point at the present moment.

"But if I do not have the gift, how was I able to use the magic of my father's staff when we fought the dragon?" he demanded angrily. "How can I see through Starhawk's eyes?"

"As to the first question, I do not know. Perhaps you have some small talent for a druid's magic—much as I do—or perhaps you have something else. You have an affinity for the forest and its animals beyond that I have seen in most men. Yet you evidently lack the mystic connection to all of life that a true druid must possess."

The wizard paused. "Where Starhawk is concerned, you do no more and no less than any other apprentice wizard," he said gently. "The falcon is your true familiar."

This knowledge hit Korigan like a blow to the gut. The rapturous flight he had shared with Starhawk was not a druid's mystical rapport with animals, but a wizard's connection to his familiar.

"Then I am a wizard after all," Korigan said, dejected.

"Hardly!" Percival muttered.

"You could *become* a wizard," Brucel corrected him gently. "You have a certain amount of talent, if only you choose to develop it."

"There is no other choice in Sanderstone!"

"Sanderstone is not the world," the wizard pointed out, but Korigan was no longer listening. So Brucel helped the boy to his feet and hoisted him onto Bronwyn's back.

They rode in silence throughout the rest of the day. Despairing and bitter, Korigan resolved to throw himself back into the only thing he knew. He restrung his bow and checked the fletching on each of his arrows. As he worked, he forced himself to accept what Brucel already knew: they had to return to the original plan for this hunt. And so Korigan prepared, and thrust aside his loathing for the task before him. He was a hunter, and he would return to Sanderstone with a unicorn's horn on his belt.

13
The Unicorn's Glade

When the first colors of sunset stained the western sky, Brucel called a halt. "We will try to enter the glade now," he said. "Give me Thorn's staff."

Korigan looked around. They had been riding through a woodland meadow, and he saw nothing different or unusual in the landscape. There was a stand of oaks up ahead, but their branches were nearly bare, and Korigan could see beyond them into the forest ahead. Why Brucel had chosen this spot, Korigan did not know. The boy felt not a trace of the mystical peace that had heralded the unicorn's first appearance. But he shrugged and handed the druid's staff to his uncle.

Brucel strode to the oak grove and raised the staff to the setting sun. Little by little, sunlight gathered in a sparkling halo of light at the end of the staff. The wizard slowly swung the staff toward the oaks, then traced a large arc in the air. A shimmering doorway formed and began to glow brighter and brighter until it obscured the oak trees and the forest beyond.

Brucel motioned Korigan forward. Although the boy was not certain that the horses would take to this idea, he grabbed the reins of Brucel's horse and urged Bronwyn forward with a nudge of his knees.

To Korigan's surprise, both horses trotted eagerly toward the portal. Starhawk fairly leaped from her perch on the saddle's pommel into the air. The falcon uttered a glad cry as she disappeared through the bright doorway. Taking a deep breath, Korigan followed his falcon familiar.

When the magical light faded, Korigan found himself in a place more beautiful than any he had ever seen. Although elsewhere autumn was edging toward winter, this place was clad in the fresh colors of springtime. The terrain before him was completely different from the valley they had left behind. Instead of meadows, here were rolling hills and thick stands of trees. A bubbling stream wound around and around the hills, its music singing harmony with the nightsong of birds.

Korigan drew in a ragged breath. He looked behind him, and there stood the familiar oak trees. The trees were no longer barren, but full and green. Plump squirrels chattered and played tag among the branches.

"It is late," Brucel said softly. "We will make camp here and begin the hunt first thing in the morning."

The boy nodded and set about making a fire. Following the Travelers' example, he carefully cut and peeled back a piece of sod. He could not bear the thought of leaving a scar on this beautiful land.

The companions ate sparingly that evening from the rations that Korigan had brought from Sanderstone. Starhawk would not hunt, though she flew until the last of the light faded. Even Percival did not demand fresh game, but subsisted on dried trail food without his usual complaints.

Long into the night Korigan lay awake. When at last he slept, his dreams echoed the visions that had troubled him in the druid's pond.

Morning came far too soon, and Korigan was awakened by the squawk of Brucel's shawm. He rubbed sleep from his eyes and gazed around in disbelief. The sun was already touching the tops of the oak trees! Exhausted and heartsick as he had been, he had slept far longer than he'd intended.

Percival was crouched beside Korigan, his ears back and his yellow tail lashing. "Of all the wizards in Sanderstone, I had to get one with bardic pretensions," the cat complained. "And do you think I'm happy about this?"

Actually, Korigan suspected that Percival was quite pleased to be the headmaster's familiar. "You'll probably get used to it," he suggested.

"Huh! Not likely. If I were a tone-deaf duck, maybe. Music to molt by," Percival observed scathingly.

Indeed, the wizard's music did sound distinctively like a prolonged, off-tune quack. Brucel must have sensed their scrutiny, for he looked up. He smiled at his audience, not at all embarrassed to be caught playing the shawm.

"Good, you're awake. After yesterday's ordeal, you needed the sleep. Even so, I've been playing since dawn, and quite frankly I was beginning to think that you might never awaken!"

Percival's eyes narrowed, and the wizard turned a frown upon the cat. "I was *not* playing loud enough to wake the dead," he said, apparently in response to the cat's silent complaints.

"But loud enough to scare away game," Korigan pointed out.

The wizard waved away that observation. "The unicorn knows that we're here, of course. Since surprise is impossible, I thought I might as well pipe in the dawn. It is one of the few customs I have kept from my days as an aspiring druid," Brucel mused, "and I find it very satisfying. That's enough from you," he said in a sharp aside to Percival.

"And you know," the wizard continued, with a note of pride in his voice, "I do think I'm improving. That performance with the Travelers convinced me that I do have some small gift, after all." With that Brucel again began to play.

Percival lifted his leg and began to wash, but the wizard was too intent in his music to acknowledge the feline insult. When his grooming was completed, the cat turned to Korigan and observed, "I'll be a mountain lion before the headmaster will be a bard, you know. You humans have a remarkable capacity for wishful thinking!"

"So I've noticed," the boy responded sadly.

And on that bitter note, Korigan gathered up his bow and his quiver. He waved to his uncle and took off in search of the unicorn. As he headed into the trees, he noticed that the shawm's voice faltered and then fell silent.

Throughout the morning Korigan searched for some sign of the unicorn's passing. Evidence of her presence was everywhere, in the peace and magic that permeated the glade, yet there were no tracks to be seen. No spoor, not even a bent twig to indicate where the unicorn might have passed.

Korigan stopped at midday and ate a few wild strawberries, knowing as he did that such a meal should have been impossible so close to winter. Then, reluctantly, he resumed his hunt.

The afternoon sun was already casting long

shadows by the time Korigan found his first tangible proof of the unicorn's presence. In the soft soil near the ever-present stream, Korigan found dainty hoof prints, cloven like those of a goat. He dropped to his knees and examined the marks. There was no depression in the soil; the prints seemed to be no more than lingering shadows.

Still, they were all he had. Taking his bow from his shoulder, Korigan began to stalk the unicorn in earnest. Weapon in hand, he followed the shadowy prints along the stream.

Hours passed as Korigan tracked the elusive unicorn, and still daylight endured. For a time this puzzled him, until he realized that the days were longer here in the unicorn's glade. Just as sunrise came before he had expected it, the sun clung to the sky long after it should have set. In this magical place it was ever vernal equinox, and day and night were always in perfect balance. No brief autumn days here, or early sunsets.

When twilight finally came, Korigan noticed that he had traced a wide circle, and that he was now heading back toward the campsite. He was tired, and frustrated, and ready to give up. He was rapidly becoming convinced that the trail he had been following was no more than an illusion. This conclusion seemed assured when the trail came to a dense thicket and then disappeared.

Just a few minutes more, Korigan decided. He would see what—if anything—was on the other side of the tangle of bushes, and then he would admit defeat.

Slowly, carefully, calling upon all the skills of stealth and silence that he had learned through years of imitating prowling animals and hunting falcons, Korigan crept through a thicket. He did not make a sound. He hardly dared to breathe.

Soon he saw glimpses of a clearing beyond the thicket. Korigan edged forward until there was but a thin curtain of vines between him and the clearing. He parted the vines and looked out.

There stood the unicorn.

Korigan gazed at the magical beast for a long time before he remembered to breathe. The awe and wonder he had felt at his first glimpse of the unicorn seemed a pale thing now. At home in her own glade, the unicorn was even more wondrously fair.

Her coat gleamed purest white against the

bright, deep greens of the woodland, and her swirling horn caught the fading sunlight with an opalescent shimmer. Like a gem in a perfect setting, the creature demanded admiration.

The unicorn's head was lifted to watch a falcon's flight. Her profile was delicate, with a slender head and long, elegant ears. Her dark eyes were enormous, fringed with lashes the color of snow. A silky, silvery mane cascaded in ringlets about her slender neck, hanging nearly to the ground. Flowers had been braided into the unicorn's mane and tail, as artfully as if she had been tended by elven hands. The unicorn was magic incarnate, eternal springtime.

For a long time Korigan gazed at the beautiful creature, marveling as her joy and peace stole into his own heart. And then, he began his final preparations.

Silently he took his best arrow from his quiver and fitted it to the string. With the assurance and precision that he had won through years of practice, he sighted down the arrow at the unicorn's heart.

The unicorn turned toward him, and her marvelous eyes searched the thicket. Yet she did not move.

Slowly, Korigan lowered his bow. Why would she just stand there and let him take a shot at her? Had he done the impossible, and successfully stalked and surprised a unicorn? Many a forest creature froze before an attack, assuming that the hunter could not see them unless they were moving. Perhaps the unicorn saw him, but was following the instinct of a hunted creature.

Or did she feel safe in her hidden glade, and at ease with the presence of a young man who carried a druid's staff? No druid would harm a unicorn, and this unicorn had no reason to assume that Korigan would be the exception. Suddenly Korigan knew why Brucel did not hesitate to play his shawm in the unicorn's glade. The wizard might offend the creature's musical sensibilities with his performance, but he would not frighten her away. The unicorn knew they were here, and she trusted them. She trusted *him*, Korigan thought sorrowfully.

To shoot, therefore, would be a betrayal. Not only of the unicorn, but of all druids. His father, his mother. Korigan remembered the silent entreaty in his mother's eyes, and at last he understood what she had been trying to say to him the day he'd left Sanderstone.

Yet if he did not shoot, his mother would die. Slowly, with fingers that suddenly seemed carved from wood, he pulled back the string until it would go no farther. Korigan hoped with all his heart that the unicorn had never seen a weapon such as he now held, and that the magical creature did not understand what he intended to do.

But no, as Korigan looked into the unicorn's eyes, he saw understanding, resignation, even forgiveness. He had longed for acceptance, and the unicorn gave it, even at the cost of her life. Her calm, loving gaze never faltered. Korigan would always remember that, and it would always haunt him. The young hunter's hands trembled, but he knew that his aim would be true.

With a single quick movement, Korigan snapped the bow into position and let the arrow fly. It soared high into the sky, and glinted once before it disappeared into distant trees. He could not, at the final moment of decision, fire upon the unicorn.

She held Korigan's gaze for a long moment, and then dipped her head in a graceful nod of thanks. As silent as the arrow, the unicorn also disappeared into the trees.

The boy let out his breath in a gusty sigh. His hands shook as they lowered the bow, for he had failed, and the price would be high. Without the power of that magical horn, his mother would die. He knew that Maura would not want her life purchased at such a cost, but that knowledge did little to lessen his guilt.

The grasses behind him rustled, and Percival stalked up. For once the cat had nothing to say. The tabby went straight to the boy and wound around his legs in a silent, feline caress. Korigan stooped and stroked the cat's long yellow fur, accepting the comfort the animal offered.

Brucel appeared on Percival's heels. His eyebrows met in a stern black **V**, and his face was tight with concern. "What happened? Did you find the unicorn?"

"Yes, I saw her," Korigan murmured. With difficulty, he raised his eyes to his uncle's stern face.

"I shot, and I missed," he said simply.

That was true, as far as it went. It was all the truth he could bear to speak. He braced himself for the wizard's wrath.

To his surprise, relief flickered in Brucel's eyes. Even more surprising was Korigan's suspicion that the wizard understood why the young hunter could not fire upon the unicorn.

If that were so, Korigan thought, Brucel understood the matter better than he himself did.

The wizard placed a hand on Korigan's shoulder. "We have done what we could. Tomorrow we will return to Sanderstone. It may be that Maura has recovered her strength while we have been away."

Although Brucel's words were reassuring, his tone was not. Neither did Korigan harbor much hope. They made camp at the far edge of the unicorn's glade, but Korigan was unable to sleep for the guilt and confusion that filled his heart.

That night, as Korigan lay awake, moonlight stole into the camp on cloven hooves. As silent as stardust, as delicate as laughter, the unicorn drifted to the place where the young hunter lay.

Unable to move, Korigan gazed in wonder as the unicorn glided toward him. Soon she was close enough for him to catch her scent, which was like a meadow, like dew. Korigan ached to touch the unicorn, to speak to her and beg her forgiveness. Yet the unicorn was not looking at him, but at the gear hanging from the branches of the tree above him.

The unicorn's horn glistened in the moonlight as she raised it to one of these branches. She deftly unhooked the water flask and dropped it to the ground beside Korigan. When the boy did not respond, she nosed the flask closer to him. Then the unicorn turned and began to walk toward the stream. She paused and looked over her shoulder, clearly waiting for Korigan to follow.

Stumbling to his feet, Korigan did so. The unicorn led him to the stream and stood there, waiting. An old story crept into Korigan's numbed mind—one of the many legends he had learned in the School of Magic—and suddenly he knew what the unicorn expected of him.

He quickly filled the flask in the stream's running water and held it out to her. Slowly, with exquisite grace, the unicorn lowered her shining horn to the water. The tip of her horn dipped into the flask, and to Korigan's wondering eyes it seemed that the water took on the luminescent shine of the magical horn.

When the unicorn lifted her head, a drop fell into the flask, scattering ripples like rainbow rings through the life-giving water. For the unicorn had blessed the water.

"Thank you," Korigan whispered.

Again the unicorn dipped her head, a gracious response that was also a farewell. There was a sadness in her eyes that Korigan could not comprehend. She stepped into the shallow stream and slipped away into the night, and the water sang more sweetly where she had passed.

Sleep did not come to Korigan that night. He awoke Brucel while the sky was yet gray, so eager was he to return to Sanderstone with his treasure. Yet he could not speak of what had happened that night, for his heart was too full for words.

14
Steel and Stone

When they emerged from the shadows of
the glade's oak grove border, the companions
were greeted by a chill wind. Korigan looked
behind him. The branches of the oak trees
were again bare, but for a few clinging,
golden-brown leaves and stubborn acorns.
They had stepped back into autumn. The boy
turned his eyes to the road ahead and recoiled
in amazement.

Before him lay the moor. The burden of
fully two days' travel—and the dangers of riding through the embattled mountains—had

been lifted from their shoulders. If they rode hard, they could be in Sanderstone late the next day.

"How can this be?" Korigan said in wonder.

"The unicorn's glade is not like other places," Brucel said. "This journey has been a time of large failures and small gifts. Perhaps, despite our intentions, the unicorn has given us a gift, after all. She has placed us here to speed us on our way."

Korigan, who knew the truth of the matter, held his peace.

Apparently an autumn rain had soaked the ground while they were secluded in the unicorn's glade, for the moorland was wetter and more treacherous than usual. The riders skirted the edge of the grassy plane, searching for firm footing.

Not hampered with such concerns, Starhawk eagerly took to the sky. The falcon had not hunted in the unicorn glade, and Korigan could feel her sharp hunger. For the first time, his communion with the hawk brought pain to the young man, and he quickly severed it. This bond was not a gift of his heritage, but a rote-learned skill. Korigan might be nothing but a poor excuse for a wizard, but he did not have to be happy about it.

At last the riders found a dry path, slightly raised and strewn with rocks. The grasses on either side grew thick and high. Something about the path made Korigan feel uneasy, but he followed Brucel out onto the moor.

They had not ridden far when the hair began to prickle on the back of Korigan's neck. A silent warning beat frantically at the closed portal of his mind, demanding that he listen.

Starhawk, he realized. She had seen something and was doing her best to alert him to danger. He opened his thoughts to the falcon, and her desperate concern rushed into him. Korigan cursed himself for his selfish stubbornness, but Starhawk brushed aside his silent apology. *Fly with me, fly away from here!* came the falcon's wordless plea, but Korigan did not know how. A druid, or a wizard, might be able to change form and do what the falcon urged. He, Korigan, was neither.

He was a hunter, though, with a hunter's instincts. The boy looked over his shoulder just as three enormous green heads rose from the tall grasses.

"Trolls," he murmured, in a voice thick with dread.

Korigan had read about trolls, but once again the books of Sanderstone fell far short of the reality. The trolls were hideous things, resembling men only in such matters as number of limbs and general shape. The creatures were tall—Korigan judged them to be at least seven feet in height—and had long and twisted limbs. Their spindly arms dangled nearly to the ground, and their bowed legs gave them an odd, rolling gait. For all that, they moved with frightening speed. Clad only in greenish skin covered with warts and bumps, the trolls rushed forward, howling and shaking rough wooden clubs.

Although he knew it wouldn't help, Korigan nocked an arrow and let it fly. The arrow tore into the chest of the lead troll and sent the creature staggering back. The troll tumbled to the ground, twitching and writhing as if in death throes.

The young hunter fired again, twice, and a second troll shrieked and clutched at its blinded eyes. Korigan's next two arrows shattered the last troll's knees and felled it like a pine tree.

The attack slowed the trolls, but it did not stop them. Korigan knew what would happen, but his throat still tightened with horror at the sight before him. The troll he had shot through the heart lumbered to its feet. The other trolls were rapidly healing, too. Wounds closed, bones mended, and the trolls advanced again.

"Let them come," commanded Brucel. He dismounted and handed the reins of his frightened horse to his nephew. Then the wizard leveled his staff at the attacking trolls and waited for the creatures to come within range.

A flash of green light burst from the staff, and in an instant the trolls were engulfed in flames. Black smoke roiled into the sky as the creatures burned like oil-soaked rags. Korigan watched in horrified fascination.

"Fire is the only thing that will destroy them," the wizard said. He raised a single eyebrow and pointed with the staff toward the burning trolls. "Perhaps now you see the benefit in that unlearned lesson in throwing fire."

Korigan glanced over at his uncle, a retort ready. His eyes widened with shock. Before he could call out a warning, a huge troll sprang from the reeds. The creature raised its massive club high and brought it down on the wizard's outstretched staff.

The wooden staff broke with a thunderous crack, and magical fire exploded from the wizard's hands in a spray of colored sparks. Like festival fireworks, the sparks darted off only to explode again and again.

One of these bolts of fire caught the troll, and the monster's triumphant leer disappeared in a burst of flame.

Korigan darted forward and dragged his uncle away from the blaze. The wizard's face was red and blistered, and much of his black beard had been singed away. The worst injury, however, was to the hand that had held the staff. The fingers were blackened, curved into a lifeless claw.

"I have no more fire spells," Brucel murmured thickly, cradling his ruined hand against his chest. "I am no battle wizard, and this fight is beyond my skill. We must flee before more trolls come."

"The trolls are all dead," Korigan assured him. "There are no more."

His uncle managed a grim smile. "In this life few things are certain, but this is one of them: There are almost *always* more trolls."

Even as the wizard spoke, several of the creatures rose from their hiding place to the east and charged toward the humans, dodging patches of smoldering grass as they came.

Korigan saw death advancing, but he determined to fight as long as he could. He pulled an arrow from his quiver and fitted it to the string of his bow.

And suddenly it occurred to him that there *was* something he could do. The arrow in his hand was tipped with flint, the chunk of rock that was meant to be used in a spell for throwing fire.

Korigan lips twisted in a savage, exultant grin. He'd throw fire, all right, but he'd do it his own way.

He dropped the bow and pulled from his boots the long throwing knives that Rimko had given him. His arm pumped as he hurled all four of them, one at a time, toward the advancing trolls. The knives bit deep into the soft soil and stood upright like four corner posts of a tiny fence. Again Korigan raised the flint arrow, and he took careful aim.

The arrow sped toward the knives and

passed through the center of the tight grouping. Sparks flew as stone glanced off steel, and within seconds fire licked hungrily at the dry grass.

The lead troll could not check its advance in time, and it stumbled headlong into the flickering fire. The creature was immediately engulfed in flame, and it ran back among its fellow trolls like a panicked torch, spreading fire as it went. Shrieking and cursing, the trolls scattered.

Korigan knelt beside his uncle. The wizard's breathing was weak and labored, but he managed a faint smile.

"You have found a new way to throw fire, I see," Brucel murmured. "Your own way. Perhaps . . . that is always the best way."

"We must leave," Korigan urged him. "The moors could well go up in flame."

"You go," the wizard said in a feeble voice. "I cannot."

Korigan sat back on his heels and raked both hands through his tangle of red hair. He could not leave his uncle here to die, but what could he do?

"Excuse me, but aren't we forgetting something?" Percival said with pointed sarcasm.

"You've gone through so much trouble to find that blasted unicorn—and don't think I'm happy about it—that you'd think you might put the creature's gift to good use. As a courtesy to the unicorn, if for no other reason."

"Of course," murmured Korigan. He leaped to his feet and took from his saddlebag the flask of water that the unicorn had blessed. Carefully, he poured a few drops into his hand and smoothed it onto his uncle's burned and blistered face. Then he poured some water directly onto the wizard's hand, for he did not dare touch the charred skin. Finally, he tipped a little of the precious fluid into Brucel's mouth.

As the boy watched, the livid color faded from his uncle's face. Slowly, Brucel's breathing became deeper and more regular, and the tight lines of pain eased. The wizard's eyes flickered open, and he lifted his hands to feel his face. He held out his wounded hand before him, turning it this way and that as the blackened skin fell away like the unneeded cocoon of an emerging butterfly.

"How can this be?" he murmured in an awed voice.

Korigan lifted the flask of water. "The unicorn

came back last night, while you slept. This was her gift."

Wonder and respect flooded the wizard's face. "Then you have succeeded, after all. And once again, in your own way."

Now was not the time to exult over his successes. "Let's go," Korigan urged, and he helped his uncle to his feet.

"First, the druid's staff," Brucel requested.

Korigan got it and handed it to his uncle.

As he had in the battle with the dragon, Brucel pointed the staff at a cloud. Again the cloud clenched, brooded, and finally yielded to the druidic magic. This time, the cloud sent forth not lightening, but a steady, soaking rain.

When the last flicker of fire on the moor had melted into sodden ash, the wizard lowered the druid's staff. This time he handed it back to Korigan with no sign of regret. But Korigan shook his head.

"Keep it," he said emphatically. "I have no use for a druid's staff."

The wizard nodded his acceptance and then mounted his horse. He sat for a long moment examining his hand and wriggling the fingers experimentally.

"Already it is nearly healed. I'd feared I might have lost the spellcaster's art in this hand."

The relief in Brucel's voice surprised Korigan. "That is very important to you," he observed.

His uncle smiled. "Of course. How would you feel, deprived of your bow? A wizard's hands are his most important assets." Brucel paused a moment, as if listening. "Except for his familiar, of course," he added in a dry tone, casting a wry glance over at the cat.

"Who says that wizards don't appreciate their familiars?" Percival grumbled softly from the pillion seat behind Korigan. "They just need to be reminded of our value from time to time."

"And I'm sure you don't mind doing just that," Korigan murmured over his shoulder.

"Not at all," the cat said complacently. "I happen to be a fascinating topic of conversation."

With a grin, Korigan shook the reins over Bronwyn's back and led the way across the moor.

15

The Gift
of the Unicorn

They arrived in Sanderstone late the next afternoon and rode straight to the cottage at the edge of the forest.

Korigan leaped from Bronwyn's back and ran up the walk, the precious flask strapped over his shoulder. To his surprise, Aileen met him at the door. Her usually merry face was grave, and her moss-green eyes were bright with tears. With a sob, the girl flung herself into Korigan's arms.

As his arms tightened around his friend,

Korigan felt his own eyes filling with tears. After all that had happened, he was too late!

Aileen pulled away and wiped the back of her hand across her eyes. "I thought you might never return," she said sheepishly, as if to explain her uncharacteristic behavior. "Then when I saw you, I just . . ." Her voice trailed off, and she bit her bottom lip.

Hope welled up in Korigan's heart. "Then my mother is not—"

"Of course not," the girl finished hastily. "Oh, good heavens, is that what you thought? What a goose I am, carrying on like that and scaring you half to death!"

Aileen chattered merrily as she drew him into the cabin, quite her old self. Korigan hurried to his mother's room and brushed aside the curtain. In the few days that had passed, Maura had grown impossibly pale and fragile. She lay still, whiter than the bleached linens of her bed. The only color in the room was Maura's bright hair against the pillow, and a bunch of wildflowers on the windowsill. Someone had taken the trouble to comb and braid the woman's red tresses and to arrange the flowers in a pot.

Thomas the Healer was there, his expression more dolorous than usual and his sandy whiskers even more ragged. The old man looked unspeakably weary, but his eyes lit up when Korigan entered the room.

"Did you find the unicorn's horn? Where is it?" he demanded.

"It's exactly where it ought to be," Brucel said as he entered the room, and though he spoke softly his resonant voice filled the small chamber. "Firmly attached to the unicorn."

Thomas threw up his hands. "I swear, Brucel, you'll never quite get over those years in the forest."

"I hope that I never do," the wizard said quietly. "I learned much then, and I learned still more this time. But we can speak of such things later."

He took Thomas by the arm and drew him out of the room. Aileen cast one lingering look back at Korigan and then followed them.

Left alone with his mother, Korigan took the flask from his shoulder. He poured the water onto a cloth, gently opened Maura's pale lips, and squeezed a single drop of fluid into her mouth. Slowly, one drop at a time, he gave the unicorn's gift to his druid mother.

Finally he dampened the cloth again and bathed her forehead. He sat by her bed and held her hand, watching with quiet confidence as the color crept back into her face. When Maura's breathing grew deep and steady, he kissed her hand and then quietly left the room.

Thomas rushed up to him. "May I see the flask? Is there more water?" he demanded urgently.

With a smile, Korigan surrendered his prize. His mother was also a healer, and she would want the unicorn's gift to be shared. The old man clutched the flask to his chest, and an expression of deep reverence suffused his face.

"Forty years and more I've been a healer, and I never thought to hold water blessed by a unicorn."

"And here I've been at it a week, and I'm already ahead of you," Aileen observed pertly. "Beginner's luck, would you say?"

The old man pretended to glare at the girl. "Keep it up, and I'll send you back to your father's blacksmith shop," he threatened. In response, Aileen merely tugged at the man's sandy whiskers.

Korigan watched, bemused. "By the way, Aileen, why *are* you here?"

"She's my new apprentice," Thomas said proudly, "and the best one I've had in years. Better than Nim, that worthless nephew of mine. He took off to fight in some foolish battle over land. Fortune and glory, they promised him. Bah!"

Korigan received both pieces of news with astonishment. That Nim the apprentice healer hankered after a warrior's path was surprise enough, but Korigan had always assumed that Aileen would follow her father's path and become an artisan of magical items. Her skill at crafting clever things was already considerable.

"You're going to be a healer," he said slowly, as the idea sank home.

"All due respect to Thomas, I'm going to be a different kind of healer," the girl said firmly. "There are many ways to heal. Magic is good, and so are herbs. It's been agreed that I will spend part of my apprenticeship with Thomas, and part here with Maura. Before she fell ill, she agreed to teach me herbal lore." Through lowered lashes, Aileen cast a glance at Korigan. "I suppose she thought that someone had to preserve the knowledge."

Korigan nodded. So his mother had long suspected that he would not take her place as village herbalist and had chosen someone else to train. Now that he thought about it, Korigan could picture Aileen puttering merrily about the house and gardens, tending the villagers and playing tricks on those cantankerous souls who took themselves and their illnesses too seriously. Yes, Maura had chosen her successor well.

"How is your familiar taking this news?" he asked with a smile.

"Oh, Sarah's adjusting," Aileen said breezily. She pulled Korigan to a window and pointed out toward Maura's well. There crouched a raccoon between a low trough of water and a big pile of newly picked herbs. The little animal was washing each leaf with meticulous care and an air of martyred resignation. The expression was so like that Percival often wore that Korigan burst out laughing.

He glanced down at Aileen from the corner of his eyes. Perhaps in the spring, he would take her to the Great Druid's glade. She would enjoy the trip, and could collect herbs and wild plants that grew nowhere else. He would enjoy sharing the journey with her.

"You two go take a walk in the gardens," Thomas said, fairly pushing the girl out the door. "Gather me some more, umm, woodruff while you're at it."

"Woodruff," Aileen repeated, smiling up at Korigan. She held out a hand in invitation.

The young hunter well knew that the herb flowered in the spring, and had long ago turned to seed. So, he suspected, did Aileen. As Korigan took the girl's hand, he was filled with a sense of homecoming, something that he had never expected to find within the borders of Sanderstone.

"It's been a long time since I was that young," Thomas said, gazing wistfully out the window at the couple who walked hand in hand through the garden.

"Oh, please, Thomas. You were never that young," Brucel commented dryly.

The healer cast a startled look at him, and Brucel held up his hands in a gesture of apology. "I was just teasing, Thomas."

"Hmm." The healer studied his old friend and classmate. "Come to think of it, I do remember you used to do quite a lot of that. I thought you'd forgotten how."

"I remembered a great deal during the trip," the wizard said thoughtfully. "When Maura is well enough to be left in Aileen's hands, stop by the tower for a drink, and I'll tell you about it."

"Well, now. I do believe I'll take you up on that." Thomas started to clap the headmaster on the back, thought the better of it, and cleared his throat nervously. He brushed aside the curtain and disappeared into Maura's room, the precious flask of water that the unicorn had blessed clasped tightly in his arms.

"Thank goodness *they've* gone," observed Percival in a sour voice. "Any moment now, I expected to be swept up in a group hug, or some such indignity. This outpouring of sentiment has fairly stolen my appetite."

The wizard smiled down at his familiar. "What a shame. And what would you say if I told you I keep the tower's larder well supplied with cream and kippers?"

"I think," Percival mused, "that I'd say I've finally found something to be happy about."

16
Farewells

Korigan spent the rest of the afternoon with Aileen. His friend already seemed to know that he would leave Sanderstone, and she was just as confident that he would return. At dusk they said their farewells in Maura's garden, and Aileen hurried back to her room at the School of Magic.

Korigan returned to his mother's room, and was gratified by the change in her. She still slept, but it was a healing, restful slumber.

He settled down on the windowsill and watched over his mother, wondering if Maura had also challenged the druid's pool. After a time his thoughts turned to his own experience in the pool, and he sought the meaning of those frightening visions.

The moon was high over the gardens when Korigan finally came to his answer. To those who dared challenge the magical waters, the pool revealed which things were dearest to the seeker's heart, and it made the seeker pay a price for them. If the passage led to the unicorn's glade, then a druid he truly was. Otherwise, the frightening visions showed where he ought to go, and what he should do. The magical passage was painful and dangerous, but it seemed to Korigan that the price to be paid by a lifetime of *not* knowing would be higher still.

For the remainder of the night, Korigan did not move from the window. Thomas the Healer nodded and snored in his corner chair, his hands tightly clasped about the flask of water that the unicorn had blessed. Korigan wondered if the old man would ever let it go. Korigan's mother also slept, and her soft, even breathing assured her son that all would be well with her.

As night crept toward morning, Korigan

thought of the journey to come, and of the life in Sanderstone that he was leaving behind. When his memories ran out, he simply sat and listened to the birdsong that spoke of coming dawn. He watched as the familiar mists pooled in the gardens, and he breathed deeply of the cold, fragrant air. When the first rays of sunlight crept over the roofs of the village, Korigan quietly left the cottage and made his way to Brucel's tower. He had learned enough about his uncle to know that Brucel, too, rose early to greet the sun.

He found the wizard in his garden, peering morosely into the well. Brucel was once again dressed in his splendid robes, but in his hand was Thorn's rugged staff. Percival was there also, resplendent in a new, jeweled collar. Wizard and familiar looked up as Korigan drew near.

"You're up and about early," Brucel observed. His eyebrows rose in a questioning arch. "How is your mother this morning?"

"Much better, and sleeping still." The boy smiled. "I thought you'd be piping in the dawn by now."

Percival's tail lashed vigorously. "Those days are gone," the cat said aloud. "And I, for one, won't mourn them! Every time the wizard played that wretched shawm, I found myself looking over my shoulder to see what unfortunate cat had gotten his tail caught in a door. The accursed flute is gone, and good riddance to it!"

Korigan grinned, not at all fooled by the cat's complaints. He noted how Percival twined about the headmaster's legs, like any ordinary housecat pleased with his pet human. The cat's words, however, stirred his curiosity. "Where is your shawm, Uncle?"

The wizard smiled ruefully. "I suppose I don't need to tell you that I hadn't the gift for making music. For a while I thought that perhaps I might have a bit of talent, but Percival has managed to convince me otherwise. The time has passed for these dreams, and I'm just as happy to put all that behind me. Besides," he added tartly, leveling a stern gaze at his familiar, "I got sick and tired of the cat's complaining. To keep peace in the tower, I threw the instrument down the well."

"And do you think I'm happy about that?" Percival demanded. "Now the water won't be fit to drink!"

"Why should you care?" groused the wizard.

"You drink nothing but cream!"

The cat paused to consider this logic, and his pink tongue flicked out hungrily. "Very true, and I thank you for the suggestion. All this talk has made me rather thirsty. I'm off for the kitchen. Don't expect to find any cream left over for your porridge. If I were you, I wouldn't count on having kippers for breakfast, either." With that parting shot, Percival stalked off toward the tower, intent upon emptying the wizard's larder of cream and smoked fish.

Brucel cast a sidelong glance at his nephew. "What are *you* grinning about?" he demanded.

When Korigan chuckled, the wizard's expression softened and a wry smile lifted the corners of his mustache. "I'd almost forgotten that you also endured our friend Percival. It must give you great pleasure to see him inflicted upon another."

"I won't try to deny it," Korigan agreed. "It seems to me, though, that you really don't mind the cat."

"It has been a long time since I had a familiar," the wizard mused. "The tower had grown too quiet. And I must admit, it's refreshing to have someone around who isn't overly impressed by my position. But enough of such matters," he said abruptly. "You will be leaving us soon, if I'm not mistaken."

Korigan nodded. "Today. Starhawk and I will set out after the Travelers. They are bound for the Iceflow River, and I have long wanted to see those waters. The Travelers' way is not mine, but I can learn much from them as I find my own path," Korigan said.

"That is a good plan," Brucel conceded. "You have outgrown Sanderstone, yet you are still too young to travel alone. Although," he added with a touch of pride, "you are already more skilled in the ways of the road than most men grown. And after you have had your fill of white water and black-eyed maidens? What then?"

"I will spend much of my time in the forest," Korigan said slowly, "but I will probably return to a town often."

"Sanderstone?"

Korigan shrugged. "It's not such a bad place."

"Never thought I'd hear you admit that," Brucel said in a dry voice. "As long as it isn't the *only* place, is that it?"

"I think so," the boy agreed. "There are

many places I want to see and adventures I want to experience. Still, I would like to have a place to call home. Once, I'd hoped that might be the druid's glade, but I, too, am content to let go of that dream.

"Just look at all we learned during our trip," he said earnestly. "To our east men take sides in a war over land. Had the people of Sanderstone known more about this, Thomas might not have lost his apprentice to false visions of wealth and glory. There are goblins in the hills not more than two days' travel from here, and we knew it not. A dragon awoke, war rages in the mountains, and Sanderstone slept."

"The village needs someone who can range about the countryside and bring news of the world and word of dangers near at hand," Brucel agreed. "I have never seen the need before for such a ranger, but I see it now. In fact, *ranger* is an excellent word to describe the work you have chosen."

"Ranger." Korigan repeated the word in a thoughtful tone. "For years I have wondered what to call myself. Yes, that will do."

"Then, if you're to be Sanderstone's ranger and protector, you might have need of this."

The wizard handed Korigan the oaken staff. "It belonged to your father, and it is yours by right."

Korigan drew back, surprised that his recent failure pained him still. "I am no druid," he protested.

"Yet perhaps you will wield the staff someday, not as a druid but in your own way. Until then, I trust you will know what best to do with it."

Korigan was not so sure, but he took the staff from his uncle's hand. At that moment a falcon's shrill call drew his eyes to the clouds. High above, Starhawk wheeled and shrieked as if eager to be off.

Brucel followed the line of Korigan's gaze, and for a moment his own eyes filled with the wonder of an open sky and an unknown road. Then he extended his hand to the boy. "I look forward to hearing your reports of the world beyond this village."

Korigan clasped his uncle's wrist for a moment, then turned and strode from the garden. He had one more farewell to speak this morning.

* * * * *

Korigan found his mother awake, wandering in her garden and gently touching this plant and that as if she were greeting dear friends. Maura still looked as fragile as spun glass, and she was wrapped in a shawl against the morning's chill. She smiled when she saw her son, but her eyes held many questions. They widened in shock when they fell upon Thorn's druid staff.

Suddenly words began to pour forth. Korigan told his mother all that had happened: the discovery of his father's identity, his hopes for druid powers of his own, his disappointment, his determination to bring the hunt to its grim conclusion.

As he spoke, Korigan came to understood why he could not shoot the unicorn, and why the mystical animal had blessed the hunt. The unicorn knew the heart of a druid, even if he himself did not.

"For a short time, even if only in my own heart, I was a druid. To a druid, the unicorn holds the essence of the earth's magic, much as your potions distill the power and fragrance of a plant," Korigan concluded. "Knowing what you are, I didn't think you would want your life purchased at such a price.

"There is more," he added softly. "Perhaps only the druids remember this, but the unicorn is the magic and the mystery that all men seek. How could I destroy that?"

Silence lay between them for a long moment. "Thorn's staff suits you well," Maura said simply, but her blue eyes shone with pride.

"As to that, we will speak in a moment. First, I want to give you something I found in my father's garden."

Korigan reached into his bag and brought out the seeds he'd gathered from the Great Druid's garden. His mother took them with a glad cry, and immediately sank to her knees to plant them in the rich, loamy soil. When she rose, Korigan held out the druid's staff.

"Not long ago, I would willingly have died to claim a druid's magic. That power is yours, mother. You should be the one to use it."

Maura's smile was bright and her eyes held no regret. "Do you think that I don't?" Her hand swept over her gardens, tended and nurtured, and lush and fragrant. "What I do, I have chosen."

Nevertheless, she accepted the staff and ran her hands over the weathered oak, as if the bumps and gnarls of the wood were a beloved landscape. "I will keep this in trust for you, Korigan. In time, you may find your own use for it," she said.

After that they spoke their farewells quickly, and Korigan promised to take care on his journey and return often.

When her son had gone, Maura reached out with the druid's staff and touched the soil where the seeds lay sleeping. The rare herbs grew, bloomed, and filled the air with their fragrance. The woman smiled and pressed the staff close to her heart.

"Our son is not what we might have expected, Thorn," she whispered, "but he is everything we could have hoped for."

* * * * *

Not far down the road, Korigan patted Bronwyn's russet neck and settled in for a long ride. He sent his thoughts far into the sky until he found the mind of Starhawk. It was a wizard's skill, but the young ranger now knew that no knowledge was wasted.

So Korigan sent the falcon a mental picture of the Travelers' camp, and bid her to seek out the wanderers. Starhawk wheeled hard and began her flight toward the north. And far below, Korigan's mind and heart echoed with the falcon's shrill, glad cry.

Together, the ranger and his falcon set out to follow with the wild autumn wind.